AT HOME

Naomi May's first novel is a claustrophic portrayal of three women whose lives revolve about one absent man. Juliet, his wife, is convalescent after an operation and has just come 'home' to join his two sisters who, in the beautiful Hampstead house that is Andrew's by birthright, are waiting for him to return from his diplomatic post.

Anthea, the older sister, a woman of engulfing kindness and unspoken reproach, dominates the running of the household. Frances, the golden girl, too involved with her big brother to detach herself, leads a gay and vacuous life as a magazine journalist. Juliet, self-contained, reticent, an outsider, finds herself with too much time to contemplate the sterility of her marriage. Each woman is jealous of the others' relationship to Andrew and as they live through the months preceding his return, the strain of their enforced vigil begins to tell and their jealousies, intrigues and frustrations gradually rise to the surface.

AT HOME

a novel

NAOMI MAY

CALDER & BOYARS · LONDON

Part I

Now that it was January it was easier perhaps to see the situation in its bare essentials, not gilded as it had been on her arrival in the autumn, when the trees on Hampstead Heath had looked so ornamental in the afternoon sunlight and the house itself had seemed more inviting than even her wistful memory of the place. It was Andrew's house and as his wife she would have been correct in thinking of herself as its mistress —though she had not been so tactless as to have intimated that she was other than a guest.

Anthea had welcomed her. She had stood there at the top of the steps, her comfortable but dignified person placed centrally below the classical façade, and had looked appropriate in her setting, as though it were by natural right that she and no one else should occupy the position. Arms outstretched she had descended to kiss her, had held her exclaiming, 'Juliet, at last!' then had kissed her again, and Juliet through physical weakness had felt herself succumbing to her overwhelming maternal warmth. You have Andrew's warmth, she had been tempted to say, but was glad later that she had refrained, as it would have been superfluous to have remarked to Anthea on the connection with a brother to whom she was so selflessly devoted.

'You poor thing,' Anthea took her arm to help her up the steps, 'what a lot you've been through! It is sad to have to admit that your suffering is our pleasure —for it is a pleasure, my dear, to have you home again.' A tour of the house had followed, every room, in spite of the fact that Juliet had just come out of hospital. She had not liked to protest. The rooms were beautifully proportioned and, with the exception of Frances' room, had been furnished with conservative good taste by the older sister. When the door had opened on Frances' room Juliet had received a shock, it was so bright and modern, a wide divan bed with a resplendent Spanish coverlet, a typewriter, a record-player, many photographs of Andrew. 'This room looks down on the little courtyard,' said Anthea, 'with the fountain. It's pretty, don't you think? How the children used to love it! Jonathan used to stand there for hours letting the water splash over his little fingers. It's dry now. The bowl cracked during the hard winter after Robert died. I've been meaning to get it repaired, but, I don't know—I don't seem to get things done these days. I used to be very efficient, always bustling about doing this and that, but somehow since he died it's never been the same—these little things, they seem so unimportant . . .'

Juliet's attention had strayed to a photograph, which must have been taken before their marriage when they were still at Oxford, of Andrew and herself.

'But it's Frances!'

'Mm? What?'

'The girl in the photograph,' Juliet laughed, 'it's Frances!' She averted her eyes, suffering discomfort at her error and unable to rid herself of the image of an engaged couple.

'Oh, yes, Frances?' Anthea turned to the photograph. 'That must have been taken a dozen years ago—at least.'

'She was a beautiful girl.'

'What?' said Anthea. 'Oh, yes,' she smiled vaguely, then sighed. 'She looks exactly the same as she did when she was eighteen—she hasn't changed a bit. I really don't know what to make of her. She worries me sometimes . . . We do so wish she'd get married.'

'We?'

'Andrew and I.'

'Oh.'

Anthea for the first time gave the photograph her concentrated attention. 'She was always the little sister, you know, all fun and chatter. She's very fond of Andrew.'

'Evidently!' said Juliet, but her acidity missed its mark.

'We are all very fond of Andrew, aren't we?' Anthea grasped her sister-in-law by the wrist and led her from the room. 'We have that lovely bond in common!'

When she at last achieved the privacy of her own room, it was hardly surprising, Juliet later reflected, that she should have felt so painfully fatigued, as though that bond had become a physical reality and she had toured the house weighed down by chains. At the time she had attributed both the fatigue and a constriction of the spirit, which was to become so familiar, to her enfeebled condition, for she had been told that her operation might leave her feeling depressed. However, now that four months had passed, she looked back on those glowing autumn days with wintry doubt, as though even by the mists and mellow landscape she had been deceived. And she wondered, too, why Andrew had been so insistent that she should come to London, to a surgeon who was a personal friend, rather than that she should avail herself of the facilities in Washington. At the time it had seemed reasonable, the idea had just slipped into place. But now that it was January and when she looked out over the Heath, where there was neither light nor shade in the prevailing greyness, she wondered whether he had not in fact sent her home to die.

❧

'Andrew dearest,

'You did not mention how you had spent Christmas. We had a pleasant time here, though now that the children are growing up it is not as much fun as it used to be. They don't believe in Santa Claus any more, but perhaps this is as well as there was no one to dress up in the part. We missed you more than ever this year. Not that we don't always miss you, but Juliet's presence seems to make your absence the more marked. It seems wrong that she should be here without you and your children and I did feel it was such a pity that all the little cousins could not have been together on Christmas morning to share the excitement of opening their stockings.

'Dear Juliet is being very brave and never complains so I can't really tell you how she is though her health does seem somewhat improved. She was a great help with the children during the Christmas holidays, keeping them entertained and reading them such *advanced* books. I had thought she was rather governessy with them, asking them such difficult questions. She really made them use their minds, but they seemed to like this. Perhaps I give them too little of that sort of thing. I am beginning to feel that they are growing beyond me. I can't get used to the fact that Jonathan now hates me kissing him in public and as for Marina she spends her time trying on Frances' make-up and being so silly and provocative that I was really most grateful to Juliet for making them use their energies more constructively. When your own children reach this stage she will be an excellent mother to them, though if you will forgive me for saying so I used to wonder if she gave them the love and affection that is so necessary for the happiness of a small child. But she is certainly a most interesting person—rather beyond me I'm afraid—I'm sure she must find me very dull and homely. She is a difficult person to get close to but I must say I have become very fond of her and I am sure being the clever person she is she will be the perfect wife for you. She doesn't talk much about you but I know she must be missing you—life is so bleak and grey without one's husband—and it would be both a kindness and a duty to come home for a few weeks if you could possibly manage it.

'The weather is cold and we have dark days here. I notice it more now that the children are back at school. I always feel so sad when I say good-bye to them, I think the parting affects me more than them. Now that we are quiet again I ought to get myself organised. Your tenants in Hampshire have left for South Africa and so far we have not been able to replace them. I really ought to go and see the agent myself but it is quite an undertaking to go down there in this weather. Then there is so much to be done here in this house, it's time I got the sweep in and one of the dining-room chairs is broken and a hundred and one little things that I put off attending to during the holidays. But maybe it would be better to wait till the spring . . .'

The door opened so quietly that Anthea, who did not hear her sister-in-law enter the room, started, raising her blunt, homely hand to her throat.

'I wish you wouldn't do that! You gave me such a fright.'

'I'm so sorry.'

'You're always doing it.'

'Am I?' Juliet's smile made Anthea wonder whether she did it on purpose. 'I see you're writing a letter. Am I disturbing you?'

'It makes me nervous.'

'Oh, dear, I really didn't mean to. I'm most awfully sorry.'

'What did you say? You mustn't apologise for everything—you do it all the time. There's no need to apologise here, you know, this is your home.'

'Perhaps I feel an intruder.'

'You? Why, this house, I feel as if I had been keeping it warm for you, for both of you—and your children—all these years. It was such a shame they weren't here for Christmas.'

'Ah, I am disturbing you. You were writing a letter.'

'I was writing to Andrew. I was telling him what

a help you'd been during the holidays with the children—they're beginning to be quite a handful. It was such a tragedy that Robert had to die, they need a father. If only Andrew were here . . .'

'Oh, I wouldn't hope for that.'

'You sound bitter. Tell me, dear, I don't want to sound interfering, but are you—you and Andrew, are you happy together?'

'Would it please you if we weren't?'

'What, dear?'

'I thought you must be writing to Andrew. He says you write such long, long letters.'

'Does he? Oh . . . I suppose I bore him. Yes, perhaps I do bore him. But still he ought to know, he ought to be kept in touch, as after all this is his home. Does he think of it, this house, as his home?'

'He does have thoughts on the subject.'

'Juliet, my dear, are you tired? You don't seem quite yourself. Perhaps you're not happy here, it must be dull for you. Ah, *I know*, you're missing Andrew!' She leaned forward and touched Juliet's hand. 'I know how you feel.'

'Do you?' She saw Anthea's blue eyes, which had moistened, become opaque, and as the pressure from her hand intensified, but not with affection, she sensed the three of them, sisters and brother linked against her and herself their prisoner. Why London? Why had Andrew sent her to London, to this house? 'You're right,' she murmured, 'perhaps I am rather tired today. I feel a little odd, they told me this might happen. I'm so sorry—I do hope I'm not being tiresome—a burden on you—you've been so kind.' It had worked, Anthea was now smiling, the mother, the comforter.

'I know what it is, it's the children,' Juliet's smile was false. 'The house is so quiet without them, they were so sweet.'

※

Frances was unfortunate in that she had the good looks of a contemporary ideal and every man stared at her wherever she went because every man had seen her, or something like her, before, in films, magazines, advertisements, television, and they turned to stare through shock at seeing this image made flesh.

'But where is the real me?' she asked Juliet.

'Are you worried about your identity?'

'Identity? No . . . No, not that. I'm not intellectual enough for that. I'm just a simple girl at heart really, I'm just worried about me.'

'What's wrong with you?'

'You know how to put the question—wonderful Juliet! That, precisely, is what I'm trying to figure out.' Frances, seated on the floor of her bright and gay bed-sitting-room, re-crossed her long legs in their turquoise slacks and this movement, as all her movements, was photogenic. Gaily, she asked, 'D'you think I should see a psychiatrist?'

'Whatever for? Can't you live with yourself?'

'Oh, no, that's not the problem! Problem is that no one wants to live with me—or rather, to marry me, to be more precise. There are plenty who would live with me.'

'Indeed?' Juliet raised her eyebrows, a little repelled by this directness. She said, 'But I fail to see the need for a psychiatrist. Perhaps you should consider yourself lucky that your problems are so externalised. I feel it's so much easier when one can *do* something about it.'

'You sound as if . . . Do you have problems? Not that one would know with you, you're so self-contained. Have you ever thought of going to a psychiatrist?'

Juliet responded with an unrevealing gesture.

'It's so nice to have you here, to have someone to talk to. I can't talk to Anthea, at least not about some things. It's selfish, I suppose—I'm sure you'd much rather not be here. But it does help to get it out of the system.'

'Does it help? How strange—I don't think I've ever helped anyone!'

'What an odd thing to say! Why, you've helped Andrew no end! It's the thing he always mentions in his letters, what a help you are to him, doing all that entertaining and running his life so smoothly and how nice it is having someone with whom he can talk over his problems . . . Poor Andrew, now it's me who's cashing in on that, me presenting you with my problems.' She yawned, then leaned over towards the record-player. 'So don't get a thing about it. Even Anthea finds you helpful—with the children.' Her nails, immaculate, carmine, gleamed as she lifted a record. 'I'll play something smoochy, shall I?'

Smoochy? Juliet's lips formed the word, though she questioned it in silence, and she studied the face of her sister-in-law as she listened to the palliative music. Frances worked for a smart magazine and it occurred to Juliet that the room, with its modern furnishings, its glamorous occupant, was like an illustration in the style of those magazines to an article on 'leisure and the career girl'. Then there formed in her mind's eye with the same glossy precision other images of Frances, chic and efficient at the office, or driving her sports car with the hood down and her hair blowing, or the evenings, the parties, the expensive restaurants where she would be fêted by her admirers.

'Perhaps your life is too agreeable, perhaps you don't want it changed. Why should you want marriage?'

'Oh, Juliet! Don't be so obtuse . . . No one *wants* to marry me—that's what!'

'But I don't understand. A lovely girl like you, you have everything—most things—I should have thought.'

'You can ask me again. It's what I keep saying myself—why? why? I think I really will have to see a psychiatrist—or something.' She changed the record, then leaned back against her bed, again rapt, looking smoochy, her body swaying a little in time to the music.

'Does *that* help?'

'Help?' Frances started from her reverie. 'Help what?'

Juliet lowered her eyes, lowered her voice to a stage whisper, 'Does anything help?'

❃

'What d'you think of Juliet?' Frances asked her sister. 'Do you like her?'

'She's much more intelligent than I am.'

'Yes. Well . . . I mean—what I mean is I know she's intelligent. But that's not what I asked you.

D'you like her?'

'She's Andrew's wife.'

'She's Andrew's wife—I know that, too. But what difference does that make?'

'It makes all the difference.'

'Anthea! You are so frustrating! I suppose you feel it's your duty to like her?'

'It's my duty to try.'

'And do you?' Frances waited, but there was no response. 'Well, if you're not going to say it, I suppose it'll be left to me. I don't know that I do like her.'

'I don't see what you can have against her. She's tried very hard to fit in and it can't have been easy so far away from her husband, her home. I've tried to make her feel at home here, but of course it's not *her* home.'

'Oh, yes, I know. Poor thing—all that! But there's something about her that makes me uneasy. She says such odd things, it sends shivers down my spine!'

'Now, dear, you must try to be a little more tolerant. You should remember that she has just had,' Anthea lowered her voice, 'she's had that operation.'

'Hysterectomy? Yes, that does fit. Very young really. What age is she? Thirty-five? Do you suppose she can be feeling prematurely menopausal?'

Anthea, who did not like these things to be referred to with such baldness, inhaled profoundly, after which her whole body appeared puffed out as though literally swollen with indignation.

Frances, noting this with pleasure, for indeed she had intended the effect, said, "Now, tell me one thing, just one, but you must answer honestly—why did you ask her here in the first place?'

Ruffled, Anthea said, 'You do ask the most stupid questions! Why, it was the only kind . . .'

'Oh, you're kindness itself—we're all well aware of the fact. But why . . . You and Andrew planned this between you, didn't you?'

'Yes, we did think it the suitable . . .'

'You were hand in glove!'

'Really, Frances, you make me lose patience at times! Why shouldn't he have arranged it with me? After all, I am the older sister. The house is in my care.'

'All right, well, we'll leave that one for the moment. But what I really wanted to know was why were you so keen? It's quite something to have another person in the house for months on end, particularly when you have nothing in common with them. Are you sure that there wasn't some ulterior motive?'

Anthea's eyes widened with incomprehension. Then her expression changed and she smiled benignly, 'Yes, as a matter of fact I did hope that with Juliet here Andrew might be tempted to return home for a while.'

'A hostage? Well! I hadn't thought of that one!' Frances clasped her hands behind her head against her long, smooth, black hair and smiled showing perfect teeth. 'You know you needn't have been so cagey with me. I, too, would like Andrew to return. Oh, I would! I would! Andrew, my love, come home!' She frowned, sensing a flaw, 'But there's one other thing . . .'

'Yes, dear?'

'Why was Andrew so keen that she should come here?'

'Darling Andrew,

'Today I write to you full of the joys as I have received two proposals (honourable!) in one week. So life looks up! To be quite honest I was wondering if it was ever going to happen—it's years since anyone suggested *that* to me—and since my thirtieth birthday I've been haunted by gloomy thoughts on the subject. The only blot on this sunny landscape is that, while I am ever so fond of them both, I couldn't face marriage with either of them. Which is a shame, you'll admit. Juliet thinks it's me, that I don't want to get married, that why no one proposed it was because I was unconsciously keeping them at a distance. Well, she's wrong and isn't that nice? I suspect she really thinks I am very vain and only want the admiration. Wrong again! (I do like that of course, but equally of course it's not everything, not by a long, long way.)

'My problem is that I can't get interested in the right good-husband-and-father type. So there she is right and perhaps there *is* something wrong with me. And sad to say I am hopelessly enamoured of Another (the wrong type) one Howard by name. Not interested in matrimony needless to say. His principal charm is his splendid good looks and in this (tall, dark, with *fascinating* eyes) he reminds me of you, though he's not a patch in other ways. In fact as a personality he is really a dead loss and no one can understand why I think he's so super. Could it be just an illusory resemblance to you? Oh, Andrew, if only you were here! I am so badly in need of a mentor and guide.

'Is there a hope of your visiting these shores? Anthea seemed to think you might—though I must say you've never mentioned it in your letters. But perhaps she is in a position of privilege and is given inside information as to your movements.

'I must say things are getting pretty intolerable here. Maybe it's the winter—the weather is foul—but we all in different ways seem to be at a dead end, marking time, waiting. For what? Maybe your return. Why don't you do the knight errant and release us? Poor Juliet—it must be ghastly for her, an ocean away from all her friends, marooned with nothing to do. She tries to help Anthea in the house, but A won't let her. Anyway there is nothing to do as with Annie and Mrs. B constantly at it the house more or less runs itself. I sometimes see her walking alone by the Highgate ponds with a look on her face that I can only describe as *sombre*. What can she be thinking about? She's an enigma, your Juliet—such a good listener, but one never really learns much about her. Anyway I do think you might have pity on the poor thing—she *is* your wife.

'From my window I can see the fountain in the courtyard, so dry and apologetic-looking—like an old maid. D'you remember when we were children how charming it looked with its jet of water splashing and scintillating—summer without end! But mustn't be nostalgic. (Behold sobering warning in Anthea!) It's an indictment to think that I've spent most of my life in this house—I sometimes wonder if I'll die here. Still I do wish Anthea would get the fountain mended. She's always talking about it, but never actually does it. Very lazy really, though she imagines she's terribly busy, always fussing about like an old hen and in fact doing nothing at all. But nothing! I don't know how she stands it. And the devilish thing is that she's forced

Juliet to be the same, which I am sure must be torture for her as she doesn't strike me as at all that type. One thing about this room (my all-purpose bedroom) is that at least I have an oasis, somewhere I can escape from the influence of our dear sister—that claustrophobic kindness, the unspoken reproach, the emptiness and inertia that is somehow more powerful than my ever so bright and active modus viv . . . I don't know what it is, but, though she sits around doing absolutely nothing most of the time, she has a way of making one feel that anything one does oneself, one's own interests and occupation are quite meaningless and a waste of time. One thing about Juliet, at least she doesn't think that children and domesticity are the only things in a woman's life . . .'

❊

'My dear Andrew . . .'

She should write to him, Juliet told herself, by now he would be worried about her silence. And *they* wrote so often, she was always finding them at it, rather furtively, covering the pages with a magazine or sealing an envelope, Frances hurrying out to the street letter-box, Anthea slipping the letter to Mrs. B on her day off. If they wrote to him, she, too, must write. But what could she say? How could you have done this to me? Did you mean to be so cruel? Why don't you come? Or why don't you ask me to come to you— the next boat, the next plane? She would have packed at once.

But the longed for, now, perhaps, dreaded invitation had not been expressed. His letters were all the same, it might have been one letter, friendly, full of information about his work, their friends, the children. She did not want information; she did not want to know about his work, was no longer interested; and mention of their friends merely underlined her loneliness. Then the children . . . Was it here that she felt it most, a numb spot, this sense of alienation?

For it was in London, in the home Andrew had so often talked about and to which he hoped one day to return, claiming his birth-right, that she felt truly an alien. She had felt this at all times, ever since she could remember, an unease that was both within herself and in her relations with others, but in the past it had not mattered so much, there had been distractions and always the hope that at the next stage—whether it had been gaining her degree, marriage, or childbirth, or moving to a new country, there had always been a next stage—she would finally break the glass and walk without shame into the sunlight. But now she experienced in these dark days a winter solstice that was also of the spirit, that hope's scintillating waters were dry, would play no more. There would be no next stage.

It was curious, she reflected, that Andrew with his successful career and his enjoyment of things American, the vigour, the freshness, even the vulgarity, had felt an exile in the States, whereas she, so uncompromisingly English, had been content. She had enjoyed the life in Washington. People had respected her for her Englishness, admiring, if also a little repelled; but she had not felt any need to change herself, the expansiveness of the New World had relieved her of guilt at a personal narrowness. Where she had rejected, he had welcomed, tasted, experimented and in many ways had seemed less constrained than in his own country; even his clothes had expressed exuberance. She remembered that leather coat with its fur collar, so flashy and yet so handsome; the toughness and vivacity of his conversation, an American talking with a well-bred English accent. And yet beneath it all he had not been at ease. There was a consciousness of having resigned something of importance, which was his due and without which he would forever be lessened in stature. Was that why he had sent her home—as a private ambassador?

Or was there another reason? In London she should not have felt so alone for they had many friends here from Oxford and their early married days. During those first autumnal gilded weeks she had felt both too unwell and through Anthea's gentle mothering too becalmed to renew old contacts, but with the onset of winter the house with its lovely garden had lost its balm. She had enjoyed meeting her friends again, telling them about life in foreign diplomatic circles, boasting slyly of Andrew's success; then suddenly the boast had turned on her and she had seen them looking at her with pity—poor Juliet, abandoned—and it was only at this point that she had asked herself why he should have left her here for so long when she was quite fit to travel. Why had he sent her to England in the first place? At the time he had said that a change would be good for her. He believed in change; change for its own sake, he used to say, was beneficial ...

She should write. But what was there to write about: the empty days, the anguish and suspicion that had made her refuse invitations from their friends?

She should ask about the children, but there was a blankness, as if the children had never been part of their life together, as if she had never had any children. And in any case she knew that the children would be all right, Cara was so good with them.

It was an odd coincidence that Cara should have come from the Italian lakes, a region Andrew loved, where they had spent their honeymoon and where, on a later trip, their first child had been conceived. She had sometimes wondered whether Andrew had minded that she had not been able to be a true mother to his children. He had appeared to have accepted, even sympathised with her difficulty and it had not seemed to matter, just as he had accepted and made no issue of her physical coldness; though in a sense their marriage had never developed, it had not been impaired. And Cara had been such a godsend with her tact and gentle manners, of good family she was socially no embarrassment, a European she had not imposed on her position as an employee; and without making her feel too conscious of the fact she had made good Juliet's deficiencies as a mother. At the time it had all slipped into place so smoothly that even she with her nervous habit of self-doubt had barely questioned it.

It was only now, imprisoned in the house and by the family he resented and seeing herself through the pitying eyes of their friends, that she began to wonder whether he had been disappointed and was growing restless within her narrow boundaries, through which, unwittingly perhaps, she had retained an ascendancy over him. Had his acceptance, which had seemed so civilised, been a form of dismissal? Somewhere, she knew, Andrew was not as civilised as he appeared. In his letters he did not express love, but then she had never demanded it, in recent years had even forgotten it for in Washington she had been queen of her days.

But the whole structure had given way under her feet, and there was emptiness beneath her and within. Wombless, there could be no more children; no more first love, first marriage and the creating together of a family. She had had her chance. She had not failed because, having given nothing, she had not even started to make the effort.

'My dear Andrew,' she wrote. 'The days drag a little, but it would be ungracious of me to complain as your sister, Anthea, is so very kind. I cannot see why you should have felt her such a threat. Granted she's not exactly inspiring, but she has no serious vices and has many real virtues such as gentleness and sympathy.

'Physically, I am very comfortable. I must have become Americanised as I seem to feel the cold much more than in the past. However, Anthea, though she complains that the house is stuffy, has increased the central heating and I have become so addicted to cosiness that I hardly venture outside.

'What a lovely place this is—the rooms so harmoniously and yet humanely proportioned, satisfying both mind and eye and the body's more elementary needs. The only thing missing is life . . . I enjoyed Christmas, rather to my surprise, as the children with their clamour and irreverence filled this gap and curiously enough while they were here the house seemed more not less aesthetically perfect. I was quite sorry when the holidays came to an end.

'How are our own trio? They sent such sweet letters thanking me for their Christmas presents. I do hope they really liked them . . .'

When she had completed her letter, Juliet saw to her amazement and with a quite irrational chill of fear, a quite uncharacteristic thrill of vindictiveness, that it might, but for the phrasing, have been written by Anthea.

❖

'You are so very fortunate,' Juliet said to her sisters-in-law, both of whom were seated opposite her in the charming Adam drawing-room, 'to have a house like this and to have it in London, with prices so high and space so limited, to have such a large garden where one has all the privacy and peace of the country and yet to be able to look over the Heath and see it all there, the great city of which here one both is and is not a part.'

'Hold it!' Frances exclaimed. 'I should have taped that. Would you like to write an article on this house for my mag?'

'You mustn't say "your" *you* must say "our" house,' Anthea reproached, 'or more strictly speaking, "Andrew's house". Andrew is lucky indeed, though,' she smiled compassionately at Juliet, feeling that she perhaps needed some reassurance on this point, 'he is lucky in more ways than one. He has you,' she added, making sure that the point would not be missed.

'But honestly, Juliet, would you like to do a bit of free-lance? I'm sure I could arrange it for you. You must be bored stiff here.'

'It would be ungracious of me to complain of boredom—or to complain of anything. You have both been so sweet. You must be sick of seeing me here—I expect you wonder if I'll *ever* go.'

'Is it you who wonder?' asked Frances. 'Go on, admit it, you are bored! Why be ashamed? I'd be bored.'

'You and your career girl ways! There are many things that you don't understand,' said Anthea, 'you think you live in the centre of life—all that driving about with this one and that one and getting nowhere, and what will you have at the end of it? Nothing. You know nothing about the real things of life.'

'You think everything is family and domesticity. But think of the things you've missed out on. And in any case, what do you have now? Your children are away most of the time . . .'

'I have the house. I make a home for you all, though nobody seems to appreciate the fact. I have my children. I've had happy days, happy years, I have my memories.'

'Memories! Too right! That's all you have—and the way you go on about it, living in the past, that's all you'll ever have!'

'My happiness was real happiness,' Anthea's eyes were filling with tears, 'my memories are of real things . . .'

'If I were bored, I should feel ashamed,' Juliet changed the subject hastily, 'as it would indicate a lack of resources. After all I have time to read which is quite a luxury for me. In the States we were always so busy that I felt myself becoming quite a barbarian.'

'There you see, Anthea, Juliet does something. She

doesn't just sit around and stagnate!'

'I haven't Juliet's intelligence.'

'That's not it at all, that's an excuse—you're lazy!'

'Frances!'

'Oh, you're new to this, Juliet, you don't understand that Anthea weeps easily. It doesn't mean a thing, it's a habit. She's quite thick-skinned in spite of her apparent soft-heartedness.'

'You mean I'm used to you—you can't hurt me. In fact when you go on like this it only makes me feel sorry for you. You'd better watch it, Frances, it's a sign of being an old maid when a woman becomes spiteful. Quite seriously, dear,' Anthea added more gently, 'you can't go on like this, it really is time you settled down. You're over thirty and if you want children—oh, I do want you to have children . . .'

'It's all very well for you to talk, but who am I to settle down with?'

Juliet got up and went over to the window. 'This garden must look enchanting in the spring with the fruit trees in blossom. It's so mysterious and old-fashioned with its little paths and secret places. It's fascinating, isn't it? to think of all the other people who have lived in this house, different clothes and habits . . . I sometimes feel as if the place were haunted —so many lives—not haunted in a frightening way, but benignly.'

'Yes,' Anthea sighed, 'there has been so much life here, but now it's so quiet. When Robert was alive and the children were young . . .'

'Quite so, Anthea. Juliet and I are a poor substitute. But there it is. You'll just have to put up with it.'

Anthea, ignoring her sister, joined Juliet at the

window. 'Don't be sad, dear, we will have happy days again—when Andrew comes home. I really must insist that he brings the children home for the Easter holidays. And I'll tell you what we'll do, if Cheyncotes, our house in Hampshire, is still un-let, we'll all go down there and spend a few weeks in the country. Wouldn't that be nice? I'm sure a change of air would be good for us all . . . But I'm very cross with him,' she touched Juliet's hand, 'it's very naughty of him to have left you on your own for so long—and after all you've been through. Most unfeeling!'

Don't touch me! Juliet wanted to scream at her, then she wondered why this comfortable person should have made her feel so hysterical.

'You will persuade him,' Anthea persisted, 'you *will*, I know!'

Then Juliet saw in her eyes something stubborn and domineering under the glaze of kindness.

'Can you persuade him?' said Frances, 'can you?'

'Why ask me? You seem to think that because I'm his wife . . . Why don't you try? Blood, they say, is thicker than water. And in any case you seem to forget that Andrew fills an important position, he won't have time. It's much more likely that he will tell me to go home, home to Washington, I can't think why you should be so insistent that he should come to England.'

'Wish-fulfilment,' Frances said lightly, 'we need him, all of us. He compensates for something which we all lack—life,' she smilingly whispered in Juliet's ears, 'Andrew has life!'

❖

How true! thought Juliet, over-simplified, melodramatic, but true: the marvellous thing seen at a distance, yearned-for, unobtainable, but once seen creating a gap within the viewer and a sense of personal inadequacy . . . How odd that it should have come from Frances, who was so superficial, the journalist, the glossy girl! But perhaps she had been wrong, perhaps Frances was not superficial? In the moment when she had said that, as she had smiled Juliet had experienced a rush of hope so violent it had been painful, and she had seen the world afresh, old things become new: her husband no longer a companion, almost platonic, but something other, more princely, and in his sister not a trite glamour but beauty, grace, freedom.

She decided to leave the house and go for a walk, hoping that the fresh air might ease the insomnia which had become acute since her operation. The garden backed on to the Heath and she walked vigorously despite the dankness of the afternoon and the uninviting prospect, the grey grass and trees, the grey figures which could be glimpsed from time to time, very small, mothers with prams, lonely idlers, now and then a playful dog. She filled her lungs with the wintry air and set herself to the more constructive resolution of a problem. She had lied; of course she was bored, so bored she had hardly been aware of it, it had come on her gradually. And she had lied in suggesting that she had resources; in England she had done nothing. With her new clarity it seemed to her that she could accept her failure (for she now suddenly considered herself a failure) as wife and mother. But was that all? Were there to be no more chances? Were there not other things? It was not true, she protested, that that was the only reality in a woman's life. There must be something to which she might look forward, she was too young for such despair.

She looked back to her student days when, whatever doubts she might have had about herself, there had always been hope of the unknown. There she could resume. She knew now that the unknown of those days, the things to which she had looked forward, love, marriage, children, had been a disappointment; she had not agreed with nature and in that sense her hopes were spent. But her mind was intact, perhaps improved in that there could no longer be a call, a counter-attraction from the body. She should do research, write a thesis. On what? She reviewed her loves among the English poets and chose Blake, whose daring imagination in her youthful timidity she had found so inspiring. 'The pride of the peacock,' she murmured, 'is the glory of God, the lust of the goat . . .' Blake? No, not Blake.

'Unfair! unfair!' she said aloud, as she descended towards the city along the edge of the ponds. When she had first come to London she had been surprised by the number of people she had seen walking on the Heath, then with its golden trees so idyllic, who had muttered to themselves. But she, too, had joined the anonymous protest. Her whole being protested as she gazed into the ponds—so pretty, even in winter, the trailing willows—from whose slimy bed bodies had been dredged, amputated hands and arms, on whose banks buried under the snow one hard winter an unwanted baby had been discovered . . .

But no! It was not she who had done that. She

could not have done that! She had wanted her babies. It was afterwards, only afterwards that she knew nature to be unfair, when, in spite of the length of pregnancy, the pain of birth and the anguish after the birth, she had felt that her children did not belong to her at all, quite disconnected. And the age, too, was unfair, Freud, blight on mothers, and the impossibility of being straightforward about it all for fear of the complexes the innocent child might be developing. How she envied Anthea her simplicity and the unselfconscious, animal affection that she so naturally had been able to give her children—which Andrew, too, had given to their children.

But Cara had filled the gap. Cara had proved Freud wrong, as the children were happy and well brought-up, charming and quite interesting little people, all three of them. There had been no complexes, no difficulty. Why then should she be still tormented? In what lay her sin? She was not wicked by nature, being too self-contained to lose herself in actions either good or evil. But she had sinned and she knew it by the nagging worm, burrowing in her conscience and taking voice to cry in the night, banning sleep.

It could not be helped. It was over and could not be re-lived. She had had her chance. She must press on to the future, the next stage. She would write her thesis, would find a subject—the late Shakespeare plays and the forgiveness of sins . . .

And in any case, she told herself as she hurried homeward, leaving the ponds, ascending to the elegant building, home, tea with Anthea in the drawing-room, the fire, the little cakes freshly baked by Mrs. B, in any case she was deluded, she had been all right in

Washington, it was the winter, her operation, long absence, she would be all right again, it would pass, all things pass . . .

She hurried faster and when she entered the garden, whose windings paths, bushes, trees, whose romantic shapes became nightmarish, the furies pursued, she heard it, reminder of her sin, that cry, a baby crying disconsolately in the night, the sound that she had shut out, closing her ears, shutting all the doors, the cry for help which only she could have assuaged, from which she had fled. She was fleeing now, but the cry was louder, piercing . . .

I am going mad, she thought, as she heard the brakes of Frances' dashing little car squeal to a halt, and saw Frances emerge gay and chic. Take me away with you! Juliet wondered whether she had said this, too, out loud. Take me away in your little red car, your magic carpet. She ran towards her, longing to throw herself into the arms of Andrew's lovely sister.

❖

'Thank you, Annie.' Anthea watched the door closing, then propped herself up in bed the better to enjoy her late-night cup of tea. The house was quiet, the curtains drawn, her hot water bottle at just the right temperature. She turned to the photograph on her bedside table. 'And now, Robert, we're alone and can have a nice little chat together. I haven't talked to you all day—forgive me, my dear, I've been so busy with one thing and another. How the days slip past, so many little things, little demands on my attention, and yet it all goes so slowly time might as well be standing still . . . Ah, my dear, why did it have to end like this? Why did you leave me all on my own?

'I suppose it's foolish of me to talk to you in this way, but you're all I have, Robert, I need you, you comfort and help me. Whenever I have a problem and don't know what to do about it I know I can always come to you—I'm such a scatter-brained, stupid creature, but you always give me the right advice. It's as if you were still alive and with me in spirit, dear, though I can't see you or hear your voice.

'What was that you said?

'Oh, yes, what is my problem at the moment? Well, to be honest, dear, it's Juliet. It's rather trying having her here in the house for so long, she's not a person one can relax with and I sometimes feel it's quite a battle to remember that it is my house after all. She seems to be everywhere and she moves so quietly she's perpetually scaring me out of my wits, slipping through doors like a ghost. There's something ominous about her that makes me feel uneasy—as if she were judging me. To tell the truth if I had known it was going to be such a long time I'm not sure—oh, this is very uncharitable!—but I'm not sure that I would have asked Andrew to send her here.

'And there's another thing—Andrew. Well, he always was a problem. It was all right until he met Juliet, but after that there was nothing but trouble. Then he went abroad and it was all somehow left hanging in the air like a story that's cut off in the middle . . . But it was naughty of him, you know, not to have come to see the poor thing at Christmas. She didn't say, but she must have felt it. I'm sure it was that that made her be so kind to the children—

I've never known her to pay so much attention to her own. D'you think, Robert, that there can be something wrong? Have they arrived at a parting of the ways?

'Oh, Robert, I've had such a terrible thought . . . Can it be that he sent her over here to get rid of her, that she'll stay here with us, in this house, forever? No, Robert, no! Please, Robert, you can't let that happen!

'What was that

'Ah . . . You're quite right . . . I *am* tired and at night lying in bed alone one does get things out of proportion. And of course there's nothing to suggest anything strange, no evidence at all. How silly of me!

'Well, now, where were we? Oh, yes, Andrew. What can he be up to? He always was rather callous. I don't suppose it's occurred to him that we're all longing for him to come home—though it isn't as if I hadn't told him. But the trouble with Andrew is that he's spoiled. It all came too easily to him, he had success in everything, in his studies, his career, even with women . . . They all found him so attractive, he could have had a beauty or an heiress, but instead he married that Juliet who had no money, nothing behind her. She wasn't even particularly good-looking and as for the intelligence they talked about, in the end she didn't get a first class degree not like Andrew, she wasn't even as clever as him.

'But still that was what Andrew wanted and we were all so pleased to see the dear boy happy. And then their children, so quickly one after the other three in four years. One would never have thought it, Juliet didn't seem the type.

'Robert, I've had another thought . . . I was wondering—could it possibly be that Andrew sent her here to punish us? I know you'll think this preposterous—silly woman-talk—but I've often wondered whether he resented the way things were arranged about the house. He did love the place and it was always meant for him—and of course it is his legally. At the time he seemed to accept it, didn't say much about it except rather meanly that no price was too high for freedom. But it was an odd thing that he then decided to go into the Foreign Service as if he couldn't bear to work in London with us living in his house. I know you'll say that that was just coincidence that he had reached a point where he had to decide what he was going to do and where he was going to go. But it's such a shame, I'd imagined them living in the top flat, the bit that's hardly used now—there's plenty of room here for two families.

'But it was only fair, Robert, that we should have had the house. Daddy never loved me as much as the other two—I hadn't their spirit, I never made his eyes light up like Frances with her gay girlish ways and he was never proud of me as he was proud of Andrew —so it was only fair, don't you agree? Besides I am the oldest—I think Andrew resented that a bit. And you, being far more established and so much older than any of us, were in a better position to keep the place up. Juliet, too, hadn't the know-how, she wasn't used to luxury, poor thing, and a house like this would have been both a worry and a burden to her.

'Oh, well, it's all past, and why should we regret it? Or why should I regret it—you never lived, my dearest, to be troubled by regret. And why regret the happy years? For they were so happy. And the children, you were so happy with the children. D'you remember when Jonathan was on the way, how you used to feel him kicking against my ribs, that little body kicking and struggling for life? And afterwards—oh, the sweet swell, nothing ever was so delicious as the smell of one's first baby, the little wispy curls of hair, the powdery smell on his neck after his bath when I used to cuddle him and press my face against his soft round cheek, so plump and rosy. The first smile, the sound of him cooing contentedly in his cot when he woke up in the morning and all the birds in the garden, the pigeons seemed to coo with him. Everything singing and sparkling and the nappies every morning drying brilliantly white in the sunshine. The first word, the first step and the little hand holding so tightly to my finger . . . Oh, for us nothing in the world was more important than this little fellow! D'you remember him sitting on your knee and noticing his toes for the first time—that expression of utter seriousness as he discovered that he could make them move?

'Ah, those were the happy days, a happiness that fills and colours one's life forever and ever . . .'

'But now it's bedtime.' She laid down her cup and was about to say, goodnight, my darling, when something inhibited her. A noise? No, there was no noise. Nonetheless, it was with a sense of foreboding that she switched out the light and pulled the bedcovers up to her ears.

'Dear God,' she prayed, 'forgive me for my foolishness. I shouldn't do it, it's wrong I know to prattle like this to the picture of my poor dead husband. But it helps me, oh Lord, it helps me! I who had so much have now so little—it is Thy Will, I should not protest. But with my children growing up and growing away from me there will soon be nothing. And I have not the strength to live with nothing. I can do so much for others but nothing for myself and now no one wants the love that I have to give them.

'Please, God, let not my children become totally estranged from me. Let not the pain, the anxiety, the fears be for nothing! And the joy, oh, God, let not the joy be for nothing . . .'

There was a noise. This time she heard it quite distinctly. It was quite clear. Was it in the room? For a moment she was certain that there was someone creeping round the room, fumbling. A burglar! She opened her mouth to scream, but her voice froze and in silence she listened to the sound of a stranger fingering the door handle, very softly, attempting to enter the room without waking its occupant. Her jewels were locked in a drawer near her bed. The intruder would stand beside her, peering at her through the darkness, would breathe over her. Terrified, she listened to the creak as the door opened. She should reach out and switch on the light, confound the criminal, reach for the telephone to dial 999 . . . But she was quite paralysed. If only there were a man in the house, she wailed inwardly, Robert, Andrew . . . Andrew! she wanted to scream his name.

A light was switched on by the door and she saw Juliet standing in her dressing-gown, her face faded and white.

'You wicked woman!' Anthea leapt out of bed and shook her by the shoulders, attacking her with such violence that Juliet moaned with fear and her eyes revulsed in her head. 'You did it on purpose! You deliberately tried to frighten me! I know you and your sly, creeping ways—your words so sweet and your eyes judging me. I know what you're trying to do. You want it for Andrew, for yourself. You want to be the mistress of this house!' She shook her again and Juliet subsided against the door, infinitely frail. 'Dear God!' Anthea whispered, 'what have I done?' Juliet passed her hand over her eyes. 'Speak to me, Juliet, for the love of God, speak to me!' She pulled Juliet's hand away and patted her face in an attempt to revive her.

'I was looking for the bathroom. It's these pills I take. I couldn't sleep and I was going to get a glass of water to take some more.'

'You were looking for a glass of water? But why didn't you switch on the light in the corridor?' Anthea's mistrust was returning. 'You know where the bathroom is—you couldn't have made a mistake!'

'I'm sorry. I'm most dreadfully sorry. I really didn't mean to . . . Please—you must believe me! What an awful thing to do. I must have scared you out of your wits.'

Anthea stared at her, then very slowly she raised her hand to Juliet's face and pulled down the corner of her eye to examine the eyeball. 'Just how many pills have you taken?' she demanded sternly.

'How many?' At the alien touch Juliet's strength returned. 'I—' she removed Anthea's hand. 'I don't know,' she smiled seeing Anthea's look of horror, 'I'm not quite sure.'

'Juliet!'

'Oh, don't be alarmed, I wasn't serious. Of course

I know how many I've taken!' In that moment she realised that in fact she did not know.

'But you must be more careful. We don't want a corpse in the house! What would Andrew say? You must think of him . . .'

'Andrew? Andrew is thousands of miles away. He wouldn't even know,' she began to laugh, 'he wouldn't even have to see it.'

'Now, now, we can't have you talking like that. This won't do at all! I'll tell you what we're going to do,' Anthea put on her dressing-gown and slippers, 'I'm going to take you back to your room and see you safely tucked up and no nonsense about it.'

'You're what?'

'And from now on I am going to keep your bottle of pills and every night I'll give you your ration before you go to sleep. You're not well and Andrew entrusted you to my care, so it's my duty . . .'

'I don't know what you're talking about. I'm not a child to be tucked up in bed at night, nor am I so neurotic as to need perpetual watching.'

'Juliet, my dear,' Anthea held out her arms to her, 'what is the trouble and why can't you sleep? There must be a reason. Let me help you!'

'I don't want your help! There is nothing you can do for me!'

To Juliet's horror Anthea's heavy body slumped against her, trapping her against the wall and she could feel, uncorseted, the large maternal breasts and abdomen heaving as she sobbed.

'Oh, don't say that! I want to be needed, I want to help—please let me help you!'

'No!' Juliet looked around in desperation as she

tried to struggle free. 'No! leave me alone! You're wrong! It's *you* who needs help.'

'Yes,' Anthea clung to her, weeping pathetically, 'I do, I'm so alone, my life's so empty, it's all vanished my happiness, my joy, Robert, my babies, it's all over and nobody needs me any more. I don't know what to do with myself. You could help me, Juliet, you're so clever. Juliet, help me!'

Juliet, as trapped animals will murder to escape, felt no pity, and to the weeping woman—you useless lump of suet! she would have shouted—she said, 'You don't know what you ask—I can help no one! Don't appeal to me!'

She closed her eyes to Anthea's tears, withdrew from her heavy, warm embrace, and fled from her along the corridor with the resounding in her ears, long after she had shut the door on it and the sound itself had ceased, of a cry for help, piercing in its agony, the new-born infant's mortal shriek: help me or I die!

❖

Images of snow and sun, sun and sea, salt spray or frozen spray in an arc glistening as whoosh! and away out of sight, down the mountain, a hundred, a thousand feet, the radiant summit above higher and higher . . . Ski-ing in winter and in summertime the smell of skin under sun, the feel of sand on salt skin, Ibiza, Portugal, Tangier, so many places now that she was working on the travel section, her skin permanently tanned. And for the rest of the time London was as agreeable a place as any, particularly when she could get away at weekends and it was rare that there was no invitation. So why should she give it up, the freedom of choice—pleasure without end?

But no! Frances told herself, as she re-painted her nails, no, it would not do. The pleasure was empty, she knew it all, there were no surprises, one place reached by jet being much the same as any other, the men making the same facile compliments whatever their nationality, the same monotonous pursuit of one goal. It was not that she got no fun out of the game, not at all, for if anything a capacity for pleasure made her too easy a prey. It was the repetition and a new lack of curiosity—was this the passing of youth?—which made her feel that it would really be simpler to do the same thing with one man than the same thing with many.

It had reached a point where she felt reproached by all that was most enviable in her life. Just as travel had lost its excitement, so, when she regarded herself in the mirror, her own face seemed to have tricked her: she who was so much prettier than other girls was still single. All men wanted her—but not for long. Why?

But, getting to the heart of the matter, the real urgency was in her age. Reaching thirty had been a shock—even now she still could not quite believe it. But there it was, it had to be faced: soon the supply of escorts would dwindle and she would be left on the shelf, a spinster companion to her widowed sister. Too awful, she had to admit. If only . . .

The telephone rang. As she lifted the receiver her hand trembled. Could it be? It was.

'Oh, rapture! Howard! Hang on a moment while I

switch that thing off . . .' She got up and turned down the gramophone so that the music was merely a soft throbbing in the background. 'What bliss to hear from you! I was wondering if you'd joined the Foreign Legion. You sure you've got the right number? Was it really me that you want to call . . .?'

'Don't take offence! No, of course I don't want you to ring off! I've been hoping all evening—and all yesterday evening and the evening before—that you'd ring. In fact I'd just been bewailing the fact that my ever-so-enviable way of life was quite empty without one thing . . .'

'You think so, too? Really? Am I hearing right? Why, I never thought I'd hear you confess to feeling a lack . . .'

'Oh, but darling, I can't go to the Maxwell's party with you! I'm already in bed! You can picture me lying outstretched in my outrageously seductive purple and amber harem outfit—Liberty's best . . .'

'No, no, we can't be overheard. I've got a private line in my bedroom—that was one thing I was adamant about . . .'

'Can you come here? Oh, no, I don't think . . .'

'Yes, I gathered you were lusting after me. I'd have been a bit obtuse not to, wouldn't I? You never were one to mince matters. But I must say I do sometimes wish you wouldn't be quite so direct about it all. I don't suppose it could have occurred to you that I might be sick of people lusting for me? Why not try saying something affectionate for a change? Try telling me that you love me, for instance . . .'

'I have to say it first, do I? All right then, since you ask—I have been coming to the conclusion lately that

I do perhaps love you. I suppose it must be love,' she laughed, 'I can't think of anything else that would make me feel so wretched . . .'

'How like a man—"prove it"! To make love isn't necessarily a proof of love. You, of all people, should know that! Really, you're so very crass at times that it's no wonder my friends can't understand the infatuation . . .'

'I've already told you you can't come here and you know perfectly well why not. It wouldn't do, with Anthea and my sister-in-law in the house, and if you had any real consideration for me you wouldn't insist on something that you know would make it difficult for me to continue living here. Besides, Juliet might well tell Andrew . . .'

'Yes, I would mind very much if my "precious Andrew", as you call him, got to know . . .'

'Then, if I'm a hypocrite, I'm a hypocrite on my own terms. If you want me to upset my life to suit you, you would need to make it worth my while. What would you offer by way of compensation?' Her voice was gay, 'You never thought I'd ask that one, did you? You thought you could just carry on as before getting everything for nothing—that's what they all think. I must say feminine emancipation is the best thing that has happened to the modern male . . .'

'You can't come to this house. As you've just said, you never have been here—and you never will be, at least not as my lover . . .'

'So my family are more important to me than anything else? The rest of my life has no reality? At heart I'm a conventional little bourgeoise who hasn't the guts . . . Steady, boy! You're going a bit over the edge! Don't you see, you idiot, that there are other reasons . . .'

'Ah, you're getting warmer now! You would *not* be quite acceptable. Anthea, in particular, would feel that I was letting the side down . . .'

Frances let go of the receiver and left it hanging by the side of the bed. She could hear his voice at the other end shouting, not the words, just a sound of anger. Then there was silence. Now she had done it! As she replaced the receiver her eyes filled with tears of frustration. She hadn't realised she had touched his Achilles' heel. Of course he was common, it was part of his attraction. But he would never forgive her; and, now that she had aired the issue, she realised that Anthea and perhaps even Andrew would have opposed the marriage, not that marriage had ever been a likelihood.

The telephone rang again and she hesitated before answering. There was a knock on the door.

"Who is it?' Furtively, she disconnected the receiver. 'Come in!' Juliet entered. 'Oh, it's you!'

'I'm awfully sorry. Were you busy? I heard you talking to someone and thought Anthea might be with you.'

'Anthea!' Frances said petulantly. 'You were eavesdropping!'

'What a funny girl you are! I merely came to see whether you were still awake as I'm sick of the sound of my own thoughts. Now that Anthea has taken possession of my sleeping pills I find the nights quite intolerable.'

'Anthea took your pills . . .'

'Don't worry, I shall get some more. Though she's

quite right—I should be more careful.'

'Poor old Juliet! Well, at least insomnia is one thing I don't suffer from—though I must say,' she got out of bed and put another record on the gramophone, 'I'd much rather not sleep alone!' She turned to her sister-in-law to see how this had been received, but apart from a curious glance at the large and ornamental bed Juliet's expression had remained unchanged. 'Well, as you weren't eavesdropping, you might as well know that I have mortally offended the light of my life.'

'Oh, dear! which one was that? I find it so hard to keep track of your many admirers.'

'The only one that matters—Howard. I told him he couldn't meet the family because he was too common —or something to that effect.'

'Oh?' said Juliet, a memory stirring of Anthea's opposition to her own marriage. 'And is he?'

'Maybe,' Frances shrugged, 'though I don't know that it matters. Would you say that it mattered?'

Is she trying to insult me? Juliet wondered. She said, 'Compatibility, surely, is the important thing—particularly nowadays.'

'That's what Andrew said.'

'Well, really!'

'How touchy you are! I wasn't being personal. Oh, yes,' Frances smiled, 'I'd almost forgotten . . . You came in for it a bit, didn't you?'

Juliet ignored this and in her turn asked, 'How important is money to you? Your tastes are more expensive than the average man can afford—perhaps that's part of your problem?'

'Anthea thought you married Andrew for his money.'

'Did she? Poor Anthea, she's not the subtlest of creatures. Her own life is so bounded by material things that I suppose it's hardly surprising that she looks at others in the same light.'

'So she was wrong?'

'Why, Frances, I never imagined that *you* . . . Well, since you've raised the question I think I can honestly say that money has never been of any great importance to me.'

'Gosh! D'you know I believe you!' She stared at her, astonished. 'But Anthea's stupid. As if there weren't plenty of reasons why a girl should find Andrew attractive—he's always been my favourite pin-up!'

'Your what?'

'You despise me, Juliet!'

'I? On the contrary.'

'Well, if you don't, you ought to. You know, with you I always feel—oh, I don't know—clumsy, rather trivial. You make me feel inadequate.'

'How odd!' Juliet stared at her. 'Well, since we've raised old ghosts, it would perhaps be only fair to tell you that though money was never an issue—Andrew's far too intelligent, too generous for that—I have often wondered why he didn't marry someone more, shall we say more seductive, he had such a choice—someone more like you . . .'

'Did you?' Frances murmured, gratified. 'But looks aren't everything . . .' There was an awkward pause, during which Juliet's attention drifted to the photograph beside Frances' bed of Andrew, his arm around her shoulders, laughing into the eyes of his pretty young sister. Then, to her embarrassment she realised that Frances, too, was gazing at it. 'Tell me,' Frances asked suddenly, 'what is Andrew like?'

'What d'you mean?'

'You know what I mean.'

'Oh!' Juliet coloured. For a moment she was at a loss as to how to reply. 'I don't know what you want me to say. What d'you expect? He's a man . . .'

'Yes,' Frances, quite unabashed by the impropriety of her question, repeated, 'a man!'

'Now I know what's wrong with you! It's so simple it had never occurred to me . . . Now I can see why you've never married, why it's such a problem. I knew it couldn't have been through lack of offers—no man is good enough for you. You're in love with your brother!'

'You see,' Frances was triumphant, 'I do need a psychiatrist! You didn't believe me. You thought I wasn't interesting enough to have complexes.'

'But you're like a child! You shock me!' She saw Frances smiling as she sometimes smiled at Anthea when she had offended her sense of decency. 'Oh, no—not the business about Andrew. It's your immaturity that shocks me.'

'D'you think there's no hope?'

'Hope? Of what?' Juliet momentarily felt herself the dupe of mirage and she saw herself, the three of them their places exchanged, she, the wife, become a sister and the sister the lover.

'D'you think it will never happen? I'll never find anyone good enough?'

'It depends what you want. Keep your freedom, if you prefer it. But if you want to settle down and have a family . . .'

'You sound just like Anthea! I'd thought you were

different. But you're all the same—you married women!'

'You shouldn't sneer at Anthea, you know. In some ways of the three of us it's she who is the lucky one.'

'*You* say that!'

'Anthea speaks the truth when she says there have been real things in her life—when she says her happiness was a real happiness. She really loved her husband and children.'

'But don't you?' Frances moved closer to her, crawling in her exotic pyjamas towards the foot of the bed where Juliet was sitting. 'Don't you? If I were married to a man like Andrew . . .'

'You seem to forget that Andrew did not marry a woman like you.'

'You're being bitchy! Well, I declare—she must be jealous of me!'

'How confusing! A moment ago I thought it was you who were jealous of me.' Juliet smiled. 'But perhaps I am jealous of you.'

'Are you really?' Frances snuggled up beside her, so close that Juliet could smell her tanned, scented skin. 'Do tell!'

'You're free. You've yet to make a decision of real importance. There's nothing in your life that's irrevocable.'

'You think that enviable?'

'In a way, yes. I think the moment of freedom is enviable, the consciousness. You're fortunate in being old enough to be conscious of your freedom. Of course it is only a moment. If you let it slip, you'll become— as Anthea never tires of reminding you—an old maid.'

'I need a drink. Join me? Go on, it'll help your

insomnia.' She got out of bed and mixed two very long, very stiff drinks. 'Right-ho, then, down to business! What am I to do about it? Be my psychiatrist!'

'Oh, I don't know that I can help you there. If it's Andrew—I doubt if I could cure your obsession other than by saying that he's not so special—he's not a god.'

'I should marry?'

'If you want to.'

'But how? I've got all the things men usually find alluring: looks, sex appeal, a good earning capacity. I do all the right things . . .'

'Perhaps that's your mistake.' Juliet, who normally drank very little, felt elated, quite unlike herself. 'You should try doing the wrong thing.'

'But I've done all the wrong things too,' Frances wailed.

'All? Surely not! The ways to sin are infinite. You should try a new one, make a change.' She heard a voice, not her own voice, announcing blandly, 'Change for its own sake is beneficial.'

'Just a moment . . . It clicks! Juliet, you're one in a million!'

'What is it?' Momentarily Juliet felt transported. The room had changed and she was back at Oxford, those moments she had enjoyed most, a perpetual undergraduate wearing bedroom slippers and a thick cardigan, the intense conversations late at night in a friend's room with a cup of cocoa—only this time it was not cocoa, it was gin. 'Don't leave me out in the cold!' she pleaded. 'What wicked scheme is forming inside that pretty little head?'

'That house near Petersfield . . . You know—the

country property that's waiting to be re-let where Anthea wants us all to spend the Easter holidays? Perish the thought! Poor little me—everyone's auntie . . .'

'Well, what about the house?'

'You've never seen it, have you? It's a gorgeous place—rambling sixteenth-century manor house, but with all mod. con. When Daddy was alive we used to spend long periods in the country, but nowadays that sort of thing—at least in that style—just is not economically possible.'

'Not even for the Hasletts?'

'Don't be a bore! I can't believe that you who have been married to us—yes, us, not just Andrew, you've been married to us for long enough—should also be infected with this idea that we're enormously rich.'

'Your plan? You seem to have lost the thread.'

'Oh, yes . . .' She re-filled her glass. 'Well, it had occurred to me that I could take Howard down there for the weekend—pretend it was mine. Get it?'

'I see. Seduction by cash—or the illusion of?'

'Well, why not? Men do marry for money. And I've tried sex. Sex,' she added glumly, 'gets you nowhere.'

'Could you see it through? You have to be an artist to cheat effectively.'

'But I don't know that it would be cheating. Come to that, I don't see why I shouldn't have the house. After all I was the unlucky one. Andrew got plenty and Anthea got this house—at least in everything but law. She cheated—make no mistake about that! She made it more or less impossible for poor Andrew to lay a claim on the place.'

'But surely you share it with Anthea?'

'Good heavens, no! Not in spirit, not truly. D'you know I often feel as if I were merely a lodger in this house, as if I'd rented a bed-sitter?' She got back under the bedclothes and curled up. 'But it would be rather bliss—Howard and I living in that house . . . It's got everything—and it's near enough to London . . . I'll take him down there and I'll tell him that if he marries me . . . Juliet, don't you think that's inspired?'

Juliet shook her head. 'If you're not prepared to cheat . . . ' Abruptly she laid down her glass. 'But then why should I cheat? You're Andrew's darling little sister and this is not the sort of advice I should be giving you. That drink . . . What have you made me say? What are you doing to me? Oh, my God!' she cried, as she ran from the room, closing her hands over her ears. 'If only Andrew were here! If only Andrew would come home . . .' She had fallen into the trap: she had used the word, had referred to it as 'home'.

※

'Joy! joy! oh, joy!' Frances burst into the drawing-room where her two relatives, seated opposite one another in front of a cosy fire, were taking tea. 'Tonight we will have champagne!'

'And what,' asked Juliet 'in this joyless winter are we to celebrate?'

'Tut, dear!' Anthea, had she been closer would have patted her knee reprovingly, 'you mustn't speak like that—don't be so slow! Why Frances,' she rose to embrace her sister, 'this is such a surprise! So it's really happened?'

'It's really happened—at last!'

'When will it be?'

'He didn't say.'

'Oh, my dear,' Anthea kissed her on both cheeks, 'there's nothing that could have given me greater pleasure. I'm so very happy for you.'

'Happy for me?' Frances withdrew from the embrace. 'Why me? If anyone, you should be happy for Juliet.'

'But I don't understand . . . You are engaged, aren't you?'

'Good heavens! Did you really think . . . No, it's not that.' The light had gone out of Frances' eyes. 'Really, you make me cross at times, the way your mind runs on on one theme—you never let up!'

'Is it wrong of me to think constantly of your happiness?'

'Well, I don't know about the rights and wrongs of it, but I do wish you'd let up.'

'Dear me, we are in a difficult mood!'

'Do explain, Frances,' said her sister-in-law, 'It's not every day that we have an excuse for champagne. Not any day that I can remember . . . Do share your "joy"!'

France sat down and addressed herself to the tea-trolley, 'Gosh, I'm hungry! Beastly cold outside!'

'"Difficult" was the word you used, wasn't it, Anthea? Do have pity on us . . . We're itching with curiosity!'

Frances looked up at her, her mouth full, 'Then, scratch!' She saw Juliet smiling. 'So you think me childish? You're shocked by my immaturity? Well, thank goodness I at least . . . That's right—look at

Anthea! If Anthea knew the things you said about her behind her back . . .'

'Ring for Annie when you've finished.' Anthea with dignity prepared to leave the room.

'Hey, wait! Don't you want to know?'

'What was that? Oh, yes . . . Well?'

'It's Andrew!' Frances withdrew a letter from her pocket and flourished it triumphantly. 'He's being transferred to London!'

There was silence.

'Aren't you pleased?' She looked from one to the other. 'Why don't you say something? Isn't this the thing we've all hoped for, been longing for—that we never thought would really happen? He's coming home! Andrew—shall I spell it out?—is coming home!'

Suddenly Anthea sat down. 'Juliet, dear, would you pour me another cup of tea? This is so unexpected, such a bolt from the blue . . .'

Juliet remained rigidly still. 'Are you sure?' she asked very quietly.

'Of course I'm sure! Read for yourself!' Frances held out the letter, but Juliet did not take it. Instead she stared at the mark of Frances' magenta lip-stick, the incestuous stain on the envelope.

'He wrote to you,' Juliet whispered, 'it was you he told first . . .'

'There's been some mistake!' Anthea snatched at the envelope. 'I know what's happened . . . Frances, you bad girl! That letter wasn't addressed to you at all!'

'Watch out, you'll tear it!' Frances had not let go of the letter. 'And why should he not have written to me? Andrew tells me everything!'

'Juliet!' Anthea turned to her accusingly. 'You've been keeping me in the dark! That wasn't kind, you know. After all, I am the one who should have been told first—after you, that is. I am the one who runs the household, who has to make the arrangements.'

'I knew nothing about it,' said Juliet, 'we were both in the dark.' She saw her sisters-in-law staring at her, Anthea with slowly awakening comprehension, Frances with a naïve delight which she did not trouble to disguise, and under the pitiless scrutiny of those four eyes she felt her skin flushing darkly and in her heart the birth of a dark passion to avenge herself on her husband and on his family for this humiliation.

'Don't get so upset, dear,' Anthea sat beside her and attempted to hold her hand, 'Andrew always was unpredictable.'

'You talk as if he and I were strangers! Does a dozen years of marriage count for nothing?'

'Oh, dear, oh, dear, this is most unfortunate . . . Really Frances you must learn to be more tactful! I just can't think what possessed Andrew to . . . Sometimes,' she confided to Juliet, 'I quite despair of my family.'

'Cheer up, Juliet, old girl!' said Frances, as she returned the letter to her pocket, 'you're not in the divorce courts yet!'

❖

'Andrew dearest,

'I need hardly tell you how overjoyed we all were to hear of your transfer to London. This is indeed a great piece of news. It is wonderful to have something to look forward to and I can't think of anything that could have made me feel happier. It's created quite a flutter in the dovecote—so many plans to be made, things to be done—I think we've all become more cheerful. But then—I wonder if you'll understand this? Three women living together—even with the nicest women it's not easy. It's not natural, you know, and nature has her own way of making this felt.

'I hope you won't think me carping. As you well know, I am devoted to our little sister, and it has been a real pleasure to have been able to provide a home and be of assistance to dear Juliet in her time of need. However, your return will be quite a tonic to us and will bring a welcome breath of fresh air into our relationship with one another. It has sometimes saddened me to see the little frictions that have developed between us. Perhaps we see too much of each other, maybe we're all a little stale. I wonder now whether I hadn't made a mistake in insisting that Juliet should take no part in the day-to-day domestic arrangements. I had wanted her to have a complete rest, quite untroubled by any worries about such trivial matters. But I think I may have been wrong in this—though I was only trying to spare her—as she seems to be fretting through having so little to do. I really don't know how she spends her time. She goes for little walks on the Heath and gets books from the local library, but that isn't enough to fill the day and she sometimes looks so downcast. She used to go out occasionally, but she has stopped seeing her friends, I'm not quite sure why, and has become quite a recluse. There have been times when I have found her sitting with a book on her lap not reading it just staring out of the window. It gives me quite a turn the way she stares.

'All this will pass, of course. It's probably the winter and the dullness of her life here with us. With your return to think about I am quite convinced that she will soon be her old cheerful self again. She is such a dear person—so considerate and so grateful for all the little things one does for her.

'There is only one thing, my dearest, with which I much reproach you and which has been puzzling me ever since your letter arrived. Why did you choose Frances? Why did you tell her the news before you had written to Juliet or to me? I'm sure you didn't mean to be unkind. But I must tell you frankly—and who will tell you these things if not your own flesh and blood?—that that was a cruel, a wicked thing to have done. Juliet is very reserved but I could see how upset she was. She looked quite ill, rather as she had done when she first came here and for a moment I began to worry about her. You're not a boy any more, you can't irresponsibly pick and choose—you have a duty as a husband. Why, Robert would never, never have done such a thing to me—putting his sister before his wife in a position of confidence.

'I'm afraid, though—and perhaps there is some justice in this—that you are going to be disappointed. Frances isn't at all the girl you think she is. If she had got married and had a husband and family to look after it would have been different as she would have been obliged to learn that other people have feelings to be considered. As it is she has become so hardened, so self-centred that she is quite impossible. She thinks of nothing but her own pleasures and disappointments.

She tells me she sends you photographs of herself (I'm not surprised as she never tires of examining her face in the mirror) to show you she hasn't changed. Physically this is true—she's as pretty as ever—but underneath, oh, dear, there *is* a difference. And there's another worry. I'm beginning to understand now why she doesn't marry—I think men can see that she has nothing really to offer them, no love, no affection.

'Why I tell you all this is that when you wrote to Frances you probably had no idea how she would use your letter. It was due to her that Juliet was so upset—she *flaunted* the letter at her. I could hardly believe that my own sister could be capable of such malice. And I can tell you that it wrung my heart to see poor Juliet, whom I had been cosseting and nursing back to health all these months, looking so distraught, so unwell . . .'

Anthea folded her letter, then carefully tore it up into little pieces.

'Well, Robert,' she said to the photograph beside her bed, 'here's a fine old mix-up! Just fancy! If I'd sent that letter . . . You're right, my dear, I'm far too impulsive—my heart bled for the poor thing and I got quite carried away. But you always criticised me for this, quite rightly, you were always telling me to count ten and think it over before doing anything foolish.

'And how foolish I would have looked, with it all a mistake and Juliet's letter coming in a couple of days later. Oh, the relief! Juliet looked so altered, I was really afraid she might do something desperate, she had such an odd expression in her eyes. And I wouldn't have known what to do, what would Andrew have said to me if she had gone to extremes, if she had run off? He would never have forgiven . . . Oh, Robert, what an odd idea—how complicated it all is—but I'd never realised that I was Juliet's gaoler . . . No, protector, that's a nicer word!

'Well, it was all a storm in a tea-cup, and thank goodness for that!

'What did you say?

'Oh, yes, I know I've no business thinking such morbid thoughts, no business at all. Why, it's not as if there were even anything wrong . . .

'Of course it was careless of Andrew. He should have known—three women together. But then he's so busy, he has so many important things to do, it probably didn't occur to him, never even entered his head that something so petty . . . It was his secretary's fault—some stupid girl . . .

'So we'll just forget about it, shall we? Juliet's happy and that's the main thing. And we're all happy—it's the nicest thing that has happened for years and years. Oh, Robert, if only you were here to share our happiness! If only you could be with me to welcome him, standing at my side on the steps as he helps his children out of the taxi!

'But, oh, dear, what a lot there is to be done in the meantime before we reach that happy moment! So many plans to be made—the house will have to be completely rearranged. Now here you can help me, dear. What would be the best way? Let me see—the top floor, it hasn't been used for years, there's room there for two bedrooms and a playroom. I'll get the painters in . . . Oh, what fun that will be, choosing nursery wall-papers again! I might even buy a rocking-horse—have it as a surprise, a treat! Andrew would think that a stupid extravagance. But it's so important that they should enjoy living in London . . .

'There's that girl they have. I wonder if they'll want to keep her? I shouldn't have thought it necessary, but you never know. I'll have to tackle Juliet on that one . . . In the meantime, she'll have to sleep with Lucy, the little girl. Not ideal, but if she doesn't like it she can always leave, can't she?

'We'll share the dining-room and drawing-room, naturally. And what about bedrooms? D'you think I should give them our bedroom, or would they be content with the blue room? I don't see any real need for me to move. I'm sure Juliet wouldn't mind. She doesn't seem to take much notice of her surroundings—these intellectual women—never was much of a one for her comforts. Of course Andrew will need more space. He'll have to have a study. Now where . . .

'It is going to be just the tiniest bit congested, but I'm sure we'll manage. After all they only had an apartment in the States, they've never had a house of their own, in fact this will be their first real home. Oh, Robert, if only it could always have been like this, all of us together, happy and united . . . The only real problem will be the children's holidays—they'll be sending the little boys to a preparatory school and there's plenty of room for Lucy. But how stupid of me! There's our country house. Now that Andrew will no longer be supporting a household elsewhere it should be no problem to him to keep it up, and the children can spend their holidays in the country which will be so much healthier, much more fun for them. What a blessing in disguise it was that we never found another tenant—it all goes to show, doesn't it, that one should never complain too quickly of what seems like misfortune!

'And there should be no reason at all why there should be any problem about who runs the house, who controls the servants and so on. I know Juliet would only be too thankful to leave all that to me. I'm sure she'd much rather be doing a job or using her mind in some way. Domesticity is far too ordinary for her—I have always had the suspicion that she was never much of a home-maker.

'Yes, now that I've talked it over with you, Robert, I'm beginning to see the picture quite clearly. And what a charming picture it is! The only real fly in the ointment is Frances. Do you have any ideas about that? Ah, if only she would get married—that would be the ideal solution! But d'you know, Robert, I am now beginning to wonder if she ever will marry. These career girls, they're so full of themselves, think they've got everything and act so superior to the poor, dull housewife—and then suddenly they wake up one morning to find that they've missed it all, all the important things. And I can see it happening to Frances, happening under my very eyes. It's beginning to dawn on her, she thinks about nothing else and yet never gets any nearer. All those boyfriends, all that gadding about with nothing real developing. Of course she's paying the price for her loose-living. She thinks I don't know about it, thinks me too stuffy and old-fashioned—too stupid to see. But it's she who is stupid, as if it weren't obvious, coming home drunk from those parties with her clothes put on anyhow, and d'you remember the time when she wore dark glasses to hide a black eye?

But she's paying for it now. No man will marry a —— No, I won't say it, but you know what I mean. Poor Daddy, it's lucky he isn't alive to see it—he doted on her so!

'But there is no doubt about it, she wouldn't fit in. This is to be a family house and she just wouldn't be suitable. Besides she wouldn't be happy here, particularly now that she's got such an obsession about being left on the shelf. It would be miserable for her seeing us so happy with our children, getting on with the real business of living. And, who knows, if she were forced to leave, the shock and the change might bring it home to her, might help her to come to a decision if one of those boyfriends proposed to her. She has always been too comfortable here, has never needed marriage and a home of her own . . . The change would be good for her. I'm sure Andrew will agree with this —he never was one for letting life stand still, staying rooted in the same spot.

'But how is it to be done? How can I put it to her? With Andrew here she, too, will want to stay . . . I must ask Juliet, perhaps she will have an idea, she's sure to think of something that hadn't occurred to me. And there'll be no trouble there—not after the nastiness and jealousy that seems to have grown up between them, that painful scene with the letter . . .

'Robert, my dearest, you will be wondering why I am giving this, giving Andrew so much of my attention, it's not that he is becoming more important than you, not really, not that I'm forgetting . . . But there has never been anyone to fill the gap which you left in my life, and now—at last . . . Forgive me, my dear, but it's been so hard these long years. And the responsibility, carrying it all on my own shoulders, after your death and with Andrew abroad, the responsibility for the family, for keeping us all together and preserving the home. But now with the return of the family's rightful head Andrew will come into his own and I will be able to relax and take second place. Don't think it disloyal that I should be so delighted that he is coming home, or that I should now feel that there is a new life ahead of me and in the future there will again be happy years. Our own years of happiness were so brief compared with the long emptiness when there was nothing to look forward to . . .

'And it's not that Andrew is replacing you in my affections—he could never do that. It's something new, a different relationship. You were so much older and more sensible than me, so much more understanding, that you were almost like a second father, whereas Andrew, I think of him more like a son, a grown-up son. After all it's only natural and must have been like that all along, little girls are maternal to the baby brother, and to me he was always that, the little one, someone I had to watch over and take special care of, much more so than with Frances, with her it wasn't the same at all.

'Juliet said a funny thing to me the other day. She said, "You do know, don't you, that Andrew's hair is greying?" But I don't believe it for a minute! She'd made it up—just to annoy me. I could tell because of the way she smiled when she said it. She's like that Juliet, she has a way of saying things that sound innocent enough but it's the way she says it, a malicious twist. Oh, she's a sly one, never puts a foot wrong, never says anything really beastly—but gets it across just the same! But I'm being uncharitable, I must remember that she's been ill. And with Andrew home it will all pass—having your husband with you makes all the difference. Still it was naughty of her to have said that about his hair. I know it's not true. Andrew's hair is thick and black . . .

'There's only one bone I have to pick with him—that letter. Of course he should have written to Juliet, but why Frances, Frances rather than me? That hurt me, Robert, it was wrong of him to have done that. I know Frances is his favourite. And she was Daddy's favourite . . . That was one of the things I first admired about you, that you weren't taken in by her. Frances was a great one for taking people in, twining them round her little finger. She had such an advantage being pretty and light-hearted, beside her I was so dull. I always felt she was stealing something from me, the affection of the people I loved most—it was only with you that I felt safe. She did it with Daddy and now she's going to try and do it again with Andrew. But she won't succeed this time—oh, no! I shall see to that! This time I shall have it my way. I was rather good at that—if you had only known my dearest, but even you were not aware . . . Although I was by far the least clever, I always did get my own way.'

❖

Juliet was reassured. There had been a mistake, some eccentricity of the mail; there could be no doubt about it as her own letter had arrived only two days later. She rebuked herself for the dark emotions she had entertained, for succumbing to irrational doubts and fears during those two days, which had seemed like an eternity and now in retrospect were so brief. She resented and was ashamed of having succumbed; it was not in her nature, being an essentially rational person who prided herself on her objectivity, a spectator rather than a participant.

And now, reassured, she braced herself with optimism and common sense. Andrew's letter explained so many things. It was quite plain, for instance, that he had not asked her to rejoin him because of the possibility of a change in his own position, and, as he had pointed out in his letter, it might have tired her and been a needless expense for her to have returned to the States only at once to start packing up their belongings. As it was, Cara would see to that, sparing her unnecessary worry and fatigue.

She wondered why he had not mentioned earlier that he might be transferred, but quickly brushed this question aside lest it should destroy her new cheerfulness for she could find no explanation for the reticence in his previous letters regarding a subject of such importance. In fact she had come to the conclusion that he had not missed her, that a reunion would never occur.

She wondered about the letters he wrote Frances, in which, she claimed, he told her everything. Everything? What did that cover? Had he said something about her? Did Frances hold the clue? No, surely not—Andrew would not discuss his wife with his sister! What would he have said had he known that she had felt jealous of her? That letter—something so trivial ... In the end she had not seen the letter, she had not looked to see whether it had been dated earlier than her own . . .

Juliet laughed, forced herself to laugh out loud at her folly. She must be careful, must find something more worthwhile to occupy her time, her mind; Andrew on his return must not find her too altered . . .

'My dear Andrew,' she wrote.

'This is indeed a momentous piece of news. When will the move take place, or are the Higher Beings keeping you in the dark as usual right up to the last minute?

'I wonder how you will feel about returning to London? I, myself, was disappointed—at first, though one gets accustomed to it in time. Everything seemed so much dingier and more cramped than I had remembered it, and the people less stimulating. The latter I suppose is merely a sign of age, as one cannot forever remain as at Oxford straining to be witty and brilliant (talking nonsense I suspect!) But it saddened me to see how middle-aged our friends had become, so engrossed with domestic problems, houses, gadgets, comparative prices of this or that—a sort of humdrum comfortableness. But perhaps we all become materialistic in time . . .

'Your sisters, needless to say, are whooping with joy at the prospect of welcoming you back—Baby Brother or heroic Big Brother as fits the case. You did not mention your thoughts on this aspect . . . However, I imagine that the family will not present the same problem now that your independence has been established for so long. They certainly have great expectations and will make demands on you, and I only hope that you won't find it all too claustrophobic. I shall never forget your thrill of emancipation when we first went abroad.

'There is a curious sameness in the situation. Frances of course has grown up and has her career and poor Anthea has been widowed in the meantime—but their expectations remain the same, intensified even in that, as your father is no longer here, all their hopes are placed on you, the head of the family. The only difference is in you yourself—you have changed.

'All this is bound to show itself in connection with the house, which brings me to the question of where and how are we to live? There is much reference to the fact that this is your house, but if it would make things any easier, you can rest assured that I would be perfectly content with something far more modest, provided you were happy about it and we could be reasonably independent. Can I be of any help here? As I've told you before, my health is very much better and I have become so vegetably rooted in the one spot that I think I would enjoy house-hunting. I would suggest somewhere not too close. What about Chelsea, or one of the more pleasant areas on the South Bank, Richmond or Wimbledon, where there would be some open space for the children?

'Andrew, my love, in this our first long absence from one another I have often wondered about our marriage and your feelings for me. Perhaps this will surprise you, as we have never (thank God!) at any time indulged in analytical discussions of our "relationship". But one takes so much, maybe too much, for granted . . . I am ashamed to have to admit to you that as the gap became more prolonged I have become a prey to all sorts of doubts and anxieties—you have seemed so far away and our life together like a different world, something belonging to the past. And now that you are returning to London I cannot help thinking of the year when you first left—then for a much more humble posting in the Far East—the first year of our marriage and the contrast between then and now. I have been haunted by the fear that in some way I have failed you, that our hopes were never realised . . .

'But I am being morbid. You over-estimate me, I'm afraid. I am not nearly as sensible or as self-contained as I might appear. It has been quite a revelation to me, living in this house with your sisters, to discover how petty I have become and the extent to which I have been a participant in their little feuds and jealousies. Like them I look forward to your return as a means of personal release. Like them I have become stale and have relinquished the initiative when it comes to setting my own life in order. There is something about this house that makes one feel quite meaningless, an automaton, as if one never had and never would again breathe freely.

'I can tell you—now that the end is approaching—that, in spite of all your sisters' kindness to me here, this winter has been hell and I have loathed every minute of it . . .'

As she wrote this Juliet experienced a pang of foreboding. It was so unlike her: the bald statement, the reproach so thinly-veiled, the suggestion unequivocally expressed in black and white that their marriage might have failed, that they had become estranged. Was she tempting Fate?

She should tear up the letter. She should remain as in the past dispassionate, uninvolved, leaving to

Andrew the initiative of making the statement, if indeed such a statement were necessary. She knew that on receiving the letter he would recoil; he would see her as he saw his sisters, clinging, demanding, an iron ball chained to his ankle, preventing him forever from walking the world as a free man. Never underestimate the power of the weak, he had once said to her; vulnerable in his strength it was a quality he feared. And now she, too, had discovered the secret and was abusing its power.

But it was too late. It had to be said, no matter the risk. She had lived in a void for too long, and he had left her suspended; from his letters too much had been omitted. She had sought reassurance before, more subtly, and with equal subtlety—or could it have been indifference?—he had evaded her questions. Things were not as they were. There was something, she wished to say, that must be clarified before his return. But what? Where precisely lay the root of her uneasiness? She wrote instead:

'I had never imagined that when I came here in the autumn I was leaving America for good. It saddens me to think that I shall not be seeing our Washington friends any more, especially the—' as she listed her favourites her hand faltered and she felt herself close to tears. 'Would you say good-bye to them for me?'

❦

'Juliet! Juliet!' called the maternal voice. 'Yoo-hoo! Where are you?'

'Dead!' whispered Juliet within the privacy of her bedroom. 'Shall I pretend I'm dead? Give her a fright?'

How childish! How astonishing! Was it Anthea's influence, that perpetual mothering? One day she would find herself responding in goo-goos . . .

But she must pull herself together! After all, she was a reasonable being, an adult. It was humiliating to find herself so obsessed, dreading the sound of a footstep, a door opening, to spend so much time thinking about it, going over and over the same phrases, little slights, little irritations. And it was not as if Anthea ever really did anything to justify such hostility. She might at times be tiresome, but she was without vices, without form; there was not even a distinctive flavour to her personality. So why the panic, now, as she heard those somewhat encumbered footsteps on the stairs? Why the sense of being hunted, pursued into a trap, the trap closing?

It had got worse. Since the news of Andrew's return she had followed her from room to room, amiable, remorseless, that heavy tread, a little rheumaticky, that warmth all-pervasive like the central heating. And where could she go, Juliet, the unwilling guest? Should she lock herself in the lavatory?

She did not reply to the knock on the door. When the handle turned, as she watched the high-light on the turning knob, she felt herself preparing to cry out, stop! don't do it! don't come in! But, no! she rebuked herself, she must be patient, must preserve her self-control, soon it would be all right, soon Andrew would come . . .

'Ah, there you are!' Anthea exclaimed. 'Didn't you hear me knock?'

'You didn't give me time to answer,' Juliet smiled sweetly.

'I was wondering if you would like some coffee?' Anthea was carrying a tray with two cups. 'Mrs. B has just baked some scones—they're still warm. How lucky you are that you don't have to worry about your figure!' She laid down the tray on Juliet's dressing-table and poured out. 'If anything, you're too thin. We'll have to fatten you up a bit, otherwise Andrew will think we haven't been looking after you properly. We can't have him being greeted by a ghost!'

'Is it as bad as that?' said Juliet as she meekly accepted the coffee.

'What?' Anthea, her mind elsewhere, seated herself on the edge of the bed. There was a long silence, then she asked abruptly, 'You have been happy here, haven't you?'

'The question has a ring of menace.'

'What was that?'

'Of course, my dear—yes, I will try one of those delicious scones—why should I not have been happy? Happy, that is, in so far as it is possible in the absence of one's husband.'

Anthea glanced at her with suspicion. 'You have a peculiar way of saying things—oh, it's not *what* you say! Sometimes you worry me . . .'

'Do I?'

'You know . . . Well, yes, Juliet, dear, you do worry me—you've been worrying me quite a lot recently. You have so little to do here and I'm sure it can't be good for you. I feel, too, that it's partly my fault. I haven't let you help me when you've offered to do things in the house.'

'But there isn't very much to do, what with Annie and Mrs. B . . .'

'Not much to do? Oh, my poor Juliet!' Anthea stared at her, then shook her head. 'No, I blame myself entirely. I didn't do it intentionally—I thought it would be so nice for you to have a complete rest. But I was wrong, I can see it now so plainly. Having too little to occupy yourself with you've let things get you down, got it all out of proportion.'

'But you're mistaken. I . . .'

'I know, dear, I know. You've never said it—but Anthea knows!'

Juliet was about to protest when the unnerving question formed in her mind: *what* did she know?

'But never mind, soon all of us will have so much to do that we'll forget our little troubles. It's been a trying winter for you,' Anthea added soothingly. 'And this brings me to the subject I wanted to discuss with you.'

'The weather—all that cold and misery?'

'No, no! Our plans—our spring plans!' Anthea laid her coffee cup aside and settled herself more comfortably. 'This is something which must obviously have been in your mind, too—our domestic arrangements. When Andrew returns I was thinking that the best solution would be if we opened up the top floor and turned it into a sort of nursery flat. Oh, dear, how dirty and dusty it will be—it hasn't been used for years! Then you and Andrew will have the blue room and . . .'

'Oh!'

'You do like this house, don't you, dear?'

'Oh, yes, it's a beautiful house, but . . .'

'No "buts", I've got it all worked out. I hardly slept a wink last night thinking how this and that could be fitted in. At first I must confess I had my doubts about it, but then gradually the answers came—rather like doing a jigsaw puzzle. And now I see it all.'

'I don't think Andrew wants to live here.'

'But it's Andrew's house.'

'Oh, I'm sure he wouldn't dream of turning you out—not after all these years.'

'Now, dear, don't be difficult. Of course Andrew wouldn't turn me out—as you put it. But it's only fair that he should live in his own house. If it had been an ordinary house it wouldn't have mattered so much, but a house like this . . . Besides, there's the financial aspect. Nowadays in London a house of this size requires a small fortune for its upkeep and it would be so much easier for us all if we divided the burden. I'm sure Andrew would be only too pleased to have some assistance, particularly now that your boys will soon be reaching public school age. And this reminds me of another thing—our house in the country. As you know I have been trying to find a suitable new tenant, but so far we've been disappointed. But perhaps this is all for the best—never rail against Providence!—as with Andrew here it should be possible to keep up both houses. And wouldn't that be lovely? Just think of it, the children, all the little cousins, spending their holidays together in the country, and in term-time, if you and Andrew wanted to get away for the weekend, there it would be!'

'While I appreciate all your interest . . .'

'There! I knew you'd come round to the idea! And now we're going upstairs to have a look at the children's rooms. I don't know what we shall find up there as I haven't yet looked myself. It's lucky you're not wearing anything smart.'

She grasped her sister-in-law by the wrist. To Juliet's surprise she found that she was allowing herself to be led up the final flight of stairs.

'There! The boys' room! It will be such fun for them—the dormer window—there's always something exciting about living right at the top of a house. And what a wonderful view! Look, they will be able to see right over the Heath and then beyond that the whole of London will be spread out before them. They will be able to pick out the landmarks—over there, you can see St. Paul's. I wonder what colours would be best? There's an old wardrobe in here already—that can be painted up—but we'll have to buy some new beds and chests of drawers. Shall we go round to the salesroom or would you rather buy new furniture? I feel it would be a waste to spend too much on the boys' things— but then that will be your decision. There's only one thing—they are rather far away from the bathroom. It would be an idea, wouldn't it, to put wash-hand basins in the new bedrooms? And now,' Anthea led her through a connecting door, 'the play-room! Here we can really have some fun! Nowadays there is so much to choose from in the way of nursery wallpapers. I saw one the other day that had life-size animals on it—pandas and lions and giraffes . . .'

'But Anthea . . .'

'Now I'm going to let you into a secret. You'll promise not to give it away? It's to be a complete surprise and they've to find out themselves. Well,' Anthea took a deep breath, 'I'll tell you what it is—I'm going to buy them a rocking horse!'

'Oh, this is very kind of you—most generous—far too kind . . . But I'm afraid they're a little old for that sort of thing, except perhaps Lucy. I really don't think . . .'

'Now then, Juliet, I know you're excellent at handling adolescents, but you're not going to tell me that I don't understand the things that a little child really loves. If they would like a rocking-horse, a rocking-horse they shall have! I know, dear, you're only trying to spare my pocket—you're so considerate—but my mind is made up, and we won't say anything more about it. Well, to get back to business, there's some carpentering to be done in here—built-in shelves and cupboards . . .'

'Yes, yes, but you anticipate . . . Really Anthea, I am rather tired, I . . . This is all a bit too much.'

'Oh, no, you can't escape yet! Just one more room—in here,' Anthea led her through a second door. 'Now wouldn't this make the sweetest little bedroom for Lucy? We'll have it pink, of course, make it really feminine—a frilly bedspread . . . I know! We'll get the carpenter to make her a special little wardrobe for her dolls' clothes!'

'Preposterous!' Juliet's voice was so strangled that it was almost inaudible. You wretched woman, she wanted to shake that massive, beaming form, how dare you impose . . . Instead she said, 'But what about Cara? Where will she sleep?'

'Cara?'

'Yes, Cara!'

'Oh, her—that girl you have! Well, I can't see that there will be any real need for her, but I suppose in the meantime she can sleep with Lucy. And, if she doesn't like it, she can . . . But I'm sure, dear, that you'll find her quite unnecessary. The boys will be away at school most of the time and Lucy won't need so much looking after. Remember that you will have me to help you.'

'You're so wrong—Cara is essential!' Juliet felt herself on the verge of tears: it must not be allowed to happen, without Cara she would be lost. She saw Anthea watching her, her jaw set, her eyes patient but determined. She began to laugh, hysterically through shock and relief.

'What's the matter, dear? Are you feeling all right?'

'I've just realised that in bargaining with you like this it sounds as if I'd resigned myself—had agreed to it all.'

'There's only one serious problem,' Anthea persisted, 'and I want to ask your advice about this. It's Frances . . . There really isn't room for an extra person and besides she wouldn't fit in with a family set-up. She would be out of place here—her whole way of life is too different. It would be miserable for her.'

'You want to get rid of her?'

'Oh, that's putting it very bluntly . . . I mean, I don't want to be unkind, I should hate to hurt her feelings—after all, she is my sister.'

'But?'

'If only she would get married!'

'I wouldn't worry too much on that score. I think Frances has every intention of catching herself a husband—at whatever cost.'

'I wish I could share your conviction. I know her so much better than you do, my dear. It's gone on for too long. It might be years from now—in fact I'm beginning to feel it may *never* happen.' Anthea shook her head. 'No, we can't rely on that one. We'll have to think of some other way. What would you suggest?'

'Murder?'

'Now Juliet, dear . . . Be serious, please! I'm looking for a practical solution.'

'Murder is too impractical?'

'What was that? Now let me see . . . Come on, Juliet, you're a sensible person. Try and think of *something*.'

'What about persuading her to go and work for a year in an under-developed country? That sort of idealism is quite fashionable these days. And it would be a change—I think she's rather bored with her life of pleasure.'

'You mean it would be good for her to lead a less selfish existence? It would be doing her a kindness, wouldn't it?'

'You've taken the words out of my mouth.'

'Ah, Juliet, how clever of you—I knew you'd find the answer. Well, I shall talk to her about this. Or . . . Perhaps, Juliet, it would be better if you talked to her —she might be more inclined to listen to you.'

'You mean she would be less likely to suspect me of an ulterior motive?'

'You're being tiresome. You know as well as I do that this is a problem that must be faced. And you must remember that it is principally on your account that I am going to all this trouble. You would be the one who would be most affected by her presence here. You have already experienced—surely that incident with the letter will have convinced you—how jealous she is where Andrew is concerned. She has always hero-worshipped him, even as a little girl. Rather unhealthy, if you ask me, it's not right to be quite so attached to one's brother. But there it is. And you know as well as I do how impossible she would be. Through no fault of your own she would resent you—just because you're his wife.'

'And this would not also apply to you?'

'Juliet! What a thing to suggest! Why, of course I'm fond of Andrew—but not in that way. I know this sounds ridiculous, especially now that he is what one might describe as a man of consequence, but Andrew has always been my little brother—little Andy . . . Oh, no, Juliet! You're quite mistaken! But with me it's different, I've had a life of my own, my own husband and children, my own home. Poor Frances, you see, has nothing.'

'I see—poor Frances!' Juliet turned away from her and resolutely made for the stairs. 'You're being premature. All this planning . . . Don't overdo it, as I'm afraid you are going to be dreadfully disappointed. I can't imagine that Andrew will have the slightest intention of living here.'

'There's something I've been meaning to say to you,' Anthea puffed a little in an attempt to keep up with her. 'I hope you won't mind me being personal, but before Andrew returns, you really must find a good hair-dresser, buy some new clothes . . . Have you looked at yourself in the mirror recently?'

Juliet ran down the stairs and locked herself in the lavatory. She heard Anthea's descending footsteps, a pause, then the footsteps continuing and finally dying away. There was no call, no 'yoo-hoo'. What she had wished to say had been said and now she would be occupied with other things, perhaps fumbling through a telephone directory, looking for a carpenter . . .

Juliet left her chill sanctuary and tip-toed along the corridor to her own room where she sat beside the window, soundless and immobile, as though feigning non-existence. How intolerable it all was! She tried to think, but even her thoughts were stifled. She remembered Andrew complaining about his elder sister. She had thought him hysterical; Anthea had seemed such a pleasant, homely creature, quite incapable of causing harm, too stupid, if for no other reason, too characterless. She had dismissed, as an undergraduate's over-statement, his insistence that Anthea was Anti-Life. She has a negative power, he had said, at her benign touch every nerve is paralysed. She makes one feel like the giant in Lilliput pinned down by thousands of little threads so small they are almost invisible. No, he would not live in London, nor in England, nor anywhere near her! She had taken his house, had stolen it, but she would not steal his soul . . .

How indulgently Juliet had listened to him! He had had everything; it was not possible that someone like Anthea could have been such a threat. But she had not protested as her pride had been stung by the family's hostility to their marriage. And there had been the question of the house—she had never understood how people could attach so much importance to their material possessions. Was it status? Old Mr. Haslett had not always been so rich, in fact when enraged his accent and manners had been decidedly plebeian. In those days he had often been enraged, the very sight of her had seemed to provoke him, and she had dreaded the prospect of living in the same house as this irascible old man; for that had been the original arrangement, that, if she and Andrew were to live there, they should look after the father as Anthea, sick and pregnant at the time, was too unwell to cope.

So when Andrew had complained of his family she had been over-joyed at an excuse to escape from them and had not troubled to consider whether his fears had had any real substance.

But now, her ribs contracting painfully as she struggled for breath, she understood. Nowhere to attack, nothing to analyse . . . And yet it had happened. Why, Anthea had not even listened to her! She had just continued describing her plans detail by detail with such prosaic realism that even Juliet had seen those disused, dusty rooms re-painted, filled with children's toys, books, fishing-rods . . . How had it come about? Why had she allowed herself to be led up those stairs, taken in by it all, participating in the fantasy? For it was a fantasy. Or was it? She must do something! Even now Anthea would be giving concrete form to her hope, ordering curtains, looking through the linen cupboard to see if there were enough sheets and towels . . . She must be stopped! It was not enough to know that one was paralysed—the tiny threads must be cut, slashed through with one bold action. But what? how? where should she place the knife?

Action! she was mesmerised by the word. Thought was useless, words were nothing . . . It was even becoming a physical necessity—something bold, some form of exercise which would relieve the unbearable pressure on her lungs . . .

Andrew! she would send him a telegram, I scream! hear me! help me! She could feel it, the scream rising in her throat, and the joy, the overwhelming sense of relief, as though with the sound she might fly away escaping her tormented carcass. She rushed to the window, hearing a screech of brakes on the drive. It was Frances.

'Oh, joy!' she whispered. She threw up the window and called her name then ran downstairs to greet her.

'Well, it's nice to get a welcome,' said Frances, 'what's gone wrong?'

Juliet, who was panting noisily, paused to catch her breath. 'Your car,' she said at last, 'I love that car!'

'Really?' Frances glanced at her curiously.

'Yes, I do,' Juliet tapped the wing of the machine. 'You're so lucky!'

Frances stared at her. She was beginning to feel uneasy.

'I was wondering . . . You know that house in the country—your plan? I was wondering if we couldn't drive there together. Perhaps we could go this weekend?'

'D'you mean as a chaperone?'

'Oh, no, no! Just you and I. I mean—well, we could air the place, light a fire. You know, so that it wouldn't be too damp and depressing when you go there with the—what was his name?'

'I'm afraid I'm going to Kent this weekend.'

'Well, next weekend?'

'I don't know, I don't think that will suit either.'

'Perhaps then, if you gave me the key, I could go on my own—do it all for you?'

'Oh, no, Juliet! I don't think you should be involved in this. It's not quite—there's something not right about it.'

'Oh . . . It was just an idea.'

'You do look crestfallen. Are you so desperate to get away?'

'Yes, I would like to go to the country—for the air. I need it. I feel that it would make all the difference to me if I could breathe some clear country air.'

'Nonsense!' said Frances brusquely. 'I know what your trouble is—it's not air you need, it's a man!'

❧

Images of mist and trees, dewy grass, misty downs in the early morning at Cheyncotes, the hooves of their horses leaving a dark imprint on the grass, and veil behind veil the quiet landscape, the copses, the little hills, the golden paths luring them towards the horizon, rays of the newly risen sun. There was nothing like it, thought Frances, the perfection of the English countryside, that harmonious meeting of man and nature so gently cultivated, the right tree on top of the right hill, the church tower providing a focus, a benign full stop, the intimacy, the sudden surprising spaciousness when turning a corner, up out of the wood at the crest of a hill, a long vista . . .

There was nowhere, not the Alps, not the blue Mediterranean, nor vine nor olive under a burning sun that had such power to move her—for it was surprising how one could be moved, almost to tears, by a landscape. Did Andrew, she wondered, still share this feeling? Was he in Washington an exile dreaming nostalgically of this other Eden?

For there had been nothing like it, the happy, carefree days, the laughter when they had gone riding together through the early summer haze. The smell of the hedgerows! Even now it was in her nostrils. Before the world was awake and there was only an odd farmhand in the fields, that hidden life of nature, the animals they had surprised, a fox peering at them quite fearlessly over the poppies at the edge of a cornfield, the hares racing and racing over a bright slope . . .

They were both so young, he at Oxford, she still at school. How gay he had been, so full of plans and ideas! Nothing was real, nothing mattered, it was all in the future, in the mind. He had had such a vivid way of describing things, people, places, events, that she had felt she knew it all, every detail of his life, had talked with his friends—even his girl-friends. For he had told her all about his adventures. Together they had discussed the future, at least his future, his career, the sort of girl he should marry. Then he had produced Juliet.

How well she remembered the day when he had first brought to the house this thin, blue-stocking with her drab clothes and sharp eyes that seemed to be watching and criticising—though the criticisms were never voiced. It had been a shock. Anthea had said afterwards that that had precipitated their father's final illness. All his hopes had been centred on Andrew and he had expected him to marry brilliantly, a title or a fortune, or both. But then his whole life had been ambition, pushing up, up, up from a small root. He had taken it so personally, as if Andrew had deliberately tried to spite him.

Certainly, as far as she was concerned, it had never been the same again; it was finished. There had been no more rides, no more confidences. In time, however, she had grown accustomed to the idea of Juliet and had even found her quite amusing, though Anthea had always been too frightened of her to enjoy her company. But then there had been all the quarrels about the house and finally they had left the country. Andrew had never seen his father again. She wondered if he felt remorse.

Would they ride again? When she was mistress of Cheyncotes she would ask them down for weekends. She would have ponies for his children—for her own children. But she must not think too much of Andrew; all that, it belonged to the past. For Frances, for whom the warmth of present contact was essential, who could not sleep alone, the past was dead. It was Howard with whom she would ride, the larks carolling invisibly in the blue sky above their heads. How handsome he would look on horseback, like Andrew—that curious physical resemblance.

And what a wonderful house! It was strange that she had never thought of it before . . . One thing about Juliet, she was certainly stimulating. But it was unkind of her to have suggested that she was trying to cheat. There would be no cheating, nothing like that. She would say quite confidently: this is my house—our house. It was only fair that it should be hers. Her father, who had had so much to give, had left her so little. He had grown bitter in the last years after Andrew had left and had complained that the more he gave his children the more they expected and took for granted. In the end it was only Anthea, the dull, plain daughter for whom he had had no ambition, who could soothe him. Nonetheless, he had left both houses and almost everything else to his son. Anthea had contracted a marriage in accordance with her upbringing and was well provided for, and to his younger daughter he had said harshly, the small root showing its rough fibre, 'Your face is your fortune—use it prudently.' She had been his favourite, but, disappointed in his old age, he had resented her for the joy she had brought him. She had been Andrew's favourite, but he had abandoned her to lead his own life elsewhere.

So it was only right that she should have the house in the country. She had always, she told herself, been a country girl at heart, loving the fields, the open skies, she was the one who would most appreciate it. Besides, it was only fair as Howard could not possibly afford to buy a similar property.

Would he be tempted? He was down to earth and to the point about most things—too much so . . . But this was not the moment to lament his lack of the finer qualities. How would she set about it? Would he fall for the charm of the place? Perhaps not. But he would most certainly see it as a financial asset. She considered Juliet's offer to tidy and air the rooms before they went down. Something would have to be done if they were to stay overnight in this cold weather . . . But she did not like the thought of Juliet preceding her, opening the doors, gliding noiselessly along the corridors. It might be unlucky, she was a bird of ill-omen. Then there was the other possibility —too dreadful to contemplate—that she might think of the house in terms of Andrew and herself. For Juliet, well-endowed with the finer qualities, would assuredly fall for the charm of the place . . . But Juliet must be handled with care. Her participation was essential as she would have to rely on her for the appeasement of Andrew. Did she still have the same hold over him? Frances could not tell from his letters.

In the early days there had always been some mention, some praise of his wife, but now he did not refer to her and she knew nothing of his intimate feelings.

But she must act! There was no time to lose; it must all be accomplished before Andrew's return. What a happy thought—he would be home just in time for her wedding! She put on a record, playing it very softly, poured herself a gin, reclined languidly on her bed, lifted the receiver, dialled.

'Howard, my sweet? How surprising to find you at home! Are you ill? I thought you'd be painting the town . . .

'You're not? But perhaps you're not alone?

'You are? Better and better . . .

'And missing me? Oh, this is too good to be true! I thought you'd given me up as a bad job. When I didn't hear from you . . .

'Oh. Yes, I know, darling, it was beastly of me. I could have bitten my tongue off. I don't know what made me say it—I've been tossing and turning night after night wishing it unsaid . . .

'No, I didn't mean it. And in any case that sort of thing—background and so on—doesn't count with me. It's people as individuals . . .

'The others? My family? What does it matter what they think? Besides, my sister-in-law—such an interesting and intriguing person—she hadn't a bean, but it didn't stop my brother from marrying her, no matter what the others . . .

'Oh, you're so wrong! You've said that before, but you're wrong, wrong, wrong! My family are not the most important thing in my life. You—' did she dare? she must say it, 'you are more important to me than any of them . . .

'Yes, I rang up to apologise, and, no, that is not the only thing I wanted to say.' There was a pause. How unhelpful he was—leaving her to make all the running! 'Darling!' she twisted the cord of the receiver, 'I've had an idea. You know our house in the country . . .

'You didn't know we had another house? I must have mentioned it . . .

'Do I detect a note of greed? In Hampshire near Petersfield, and, yes, it is large, and yes again, it is—' she was lying, but no matter, it would soon be the truth, 'as a matter of fact it is my house . . .

'Normally it's let, but at the moment we're trying to find a new tenant as the last lot have gone to South Africa. But how ingenuous you are! You don't imagine "—be hung for a sheep if for a lamb", that my job alone keeps me in the style to which I am accustomed . . .

'Will I treat you to a dinner? How like you! No, my idea was about something else. As I told you the house is vacant at the moment and I was thinking it might be rather fun if we went down there for a weekend. It's the most romantic old place—converted manor house, set in beautiful country, my idea of paradise . . .

'You'd like to see it? Bliss, oh, bliss! I know you'll fall in love with it—you couldn't help it. And the stables . . .

'You don't ride? Oh, that's a blow! Never mind, you could learn. I used to ride there with my brother— we used to get up early in the morning when there was no one about. Those were some of the happiest days of my life . . .

'No, I'm not being nostalgic! The past is not more important to me than the present—and the present is not as important as the future. That in fact was why I was suggesting we should go there, so that you could see how ideal it would be for us. It's within easy reach of London, you could commute without too much trouble . . .

'Why do men always think in terms of traps? I'm not trapping you. How could I? If you don't like it, you don't have to have it—you don't have to have me . . .

'Then it's a deal! Fine! When shall we . . .

'Oh, I don't know about this weekend. I'm meant to be doing something else. Still, I suppose I could cancel, make some excuse . . .

'Yes, yes! What impatience! Well, it's nice to hear you being so enthusiastic about something. If only you could also be . . . I don't suppose you could rouse yourself to telling me that you loved me?'

※

Juliet studied her reflection in the glass. What Anthea had said about her appearance was true: her hair was without style, her face wan now that she had stopped wearing make-up, her eyes dreary. It was cruel of Anthea to have pointed it out . . . But then why should she be so suspicious? Perhaps she had meant it kindly? It was true that she had aged—even Anthea, sedate and comfortably maternal, had more bloom. It was not as if she had always been so careless; as a girl she had little flair for fashion, but in recent years, after the birth of their last child, she had become reasonably smart, cultivating, perhaps at the expense of other things, a superficial *persona*. Now, as she gazed at the mirror-image, she became aware of a reversion, the undergraduate in skirts and heavy jerseys—but with an older face.

It had not occurred to her that Andrew might be disappointed by the change, that she might even owe it to him to make the effort. Their marriage had had a different basis, books, ideas, a sharing of interests, and the physical aspect had never been of much importance. Nor had it occurred to her to wonder if he had wished it otherwise. She had regarded with condescension his interest in his own appearance, the cut of his suits, the careful choice of tie, shirt or glove. He had always been more a creature of the flesh, fond of good food and wine, and there was a warmth, an animal gloss which had made him a favourite among their women friends . . . Could it be that he was having an affair in her absence? Did that explain the evasiveness of his letters? At once she dismissed the idea: he was too discreet, too ambitious. Besides with Cara in the house it would not be so easy to come and go as he chose, for she was not an ordinary servant and he would take care not to offend against her sense of propriety.

What then, she wondered, was the explanation? In the past she might have put it down to her overwrought nerves and to the fact that she had made no reference to doubt or anguish. But his last letter had made no response at all to her desperate appeal. Had she not expressed herself with sufficient force? She looked again at his letter, the sight of which on the breakfast table had momentarily filled her with hope.

There could be no doubt that he had recognised her appeal, was aware of the situation, as the whole of the first page was given over to a lame apology. He knew his sisters were difficult, she had reminded him all too vividly of his own troubles in that quarter, but he had thought she was managing tolerably well—better than he would have done, she was more civilised, more adept at preserving herself from emotional entanglements. He was sorry that she had felt so miserable, he had had no idea, why had she not told him before? It was so unlike her to write such a letter, he had not realised that she could feel so strongly about anything. Perhaps it was the after-effects of her operation? She should go away, spend a week in Paris, Florence, have a change . . .

He still did not know when he would be returning, she would have to be patient. And, please, would she not be so quick to make plans about where they were to live, he was too harassed, had not had time to think about it, it would sort itself out, she must stop making herself a nervous wreck over something so unimportant. Perhaps she should take a part-time job, he had heard from Anthea that she did not have enough to occupy her time . . .

With that he had left the subject to discuss his work and the parties that their friends were giving for him now that his imminent departure was public knowledge. The letter had closed with the usual assurances about Cara and the children, then he had signed himself, uncharacteristically with a kiss. There was something furtive about that childish X, scrawled hastily out of embarrassment or guilt.

'Well, there it is—over to you!' Juliet said aloud. 'But you should not have bothered with the kiss. No, Andrew, that was not in good taste.' It was curious, she reflected, that he should so easily have dismissed her problems, giving her so little sympathy; it was almost as if there had never been any intimacy between them. Her wretchedness was inconvenient; would she please take a holiday and cheer up so that he would be spared the trouble of having to consider her. There was a bluntness, a quality that he shared with his sisters, though in Andrew it was tempered by his education and a more developed sensibility, but it was there, in the blood, inherited from the vigorous, self-made father. She had seen it before after the father's death when Anthea had written to him, reproaching, blaming him, and he had refused to feel remorse, claiming that, whether or not his father had approved of his marriage he had been within his rights in making his own choice and the accusation was unjust. Because Anthea had suggested that his marriage was responsible for the old man's decline he had refused to grieve for him, dismissing him from his mind. In this ruthlessness lay his strength. And yet, in those days, he had leaned so heavily on Juliet, insisting that it was through her that he had gained his freedom. He had adored her, she remembered with surprise. But then how had it happened, where had it begun, that subtle erosion? How was it that he, who had once anticipated her merest whim, could now dismiss her genuine misery with the same abruptness with which he had dismissed the memory of his father?

So he was surprised that she was capable of strong feelings, had thought her adept at preserving herself from emotional entanglements! Was he being vindictive? Was this a turning of the tables, a giving back in kind of the nothing she had given him? She had never understood why he had thought so much of her, and because she could not quite believe in his love she had inhibited him by a thousand tiny rebuffs from expressing his affection. But why? Of what had she been so afraid? Even in the moments of fullness she had been withdrawn, waiting for it to happen in the future, at the next stage. A sense of alienation, at that time, too, she had been conscious of it, the invisible barrier that separated her from the things she had most desired. Was that why she had had her children so quickly one after the other, in an attempt to anchor herself in reality? It had seemed to work. She had been happy when pregnant; it was not that she had felt that she had acquired a purpose in life, rather that the question of purpose, of what it was all about, had not occurred to her. It was only afterwards, when there had been a new life, a new personality to whom she must respond, that the void had opened. It had not been as she had thought it would be. Instead of warmth and joy she had been overcome by panic, a sense of total disconnection from the tiny child that had so recently been a part of her. That terrible crying from which finally she had fled. Then, adding to her shame, was the fear that in thus dissociating herself the poor child would in its turn grow up enclosed by an invisible barrier. She had been so helpless, incapable of creating from the void the maternal sentiment with which nature had not endowed her. How she had wished that she had been born a peasant or had lived in a simpler age where there was no obligation to experience certain emotions. Later, much later, she had realised that her anxiety was groundless, the power of life being such that, despite her limitations, the children had developed into perfectly normal, affectionate little people. She alone was the one who had suffered.

It was Andrew who had comforted the crying infants, Andrew who had found Cara. Had he felt cheated of that natural pleasure where a husband and wife together enjoy their children? Had he disliked her for her coldness? There had been no reproach, no outward sign. At the time she had been so convinced that he must resent her that she had withdrawn even further within herself, strengthening the barrier, and when, after the birth of their last child, she had become insomniac and they slept in separate beds, she had been relieved that he no longer seemed to need her, seeking a response that she was less and less able to give.

But perhaps he had not resented her. Had her withdrawal been unnecessary, her fears of her own invention? When she looked back over her married life it seemed to her that she had been consistently cowardly, at each new stage she had shrunk backwards, avoiding all risk and preserving the outer shell, embellishing it with fashionable clothes, a more assured social manner . . . But, while it was easy to see the flaws in retrospect, at the time they had not been so apparent; it had happened so gradually, had just slipped into place. And even if she had been more aware would she, could she have acted otherwise? It was in her nature, something beyond her control.

She thought of Frances, the beautiful girl with many lovers, who was so obsessed by the fear of remaining single. How enviable was her freedom and the extrovert simplicity of a problem which could be resolved by an act, a conscious decision! Frances had yet to make her mistakes. She wondered if Andrew, too, regarded her with yearning, a symbol of the early days, of hope, life. There had been that letter bearing the news of his return; she could not be certain that he had not written to her first. Why had he chosen her? He could have left it to his wife to broadcast the good news. And the other letters he wrote Frances, that intimacy that had existed between them . . . Did he see in Frances qualities that he had hoped for and not found in his wife?

'How unfair!' she said aloud. 'I am not Frances. You should not have married me if you had wanted a golden girl. I have always been as I am now, trapped by consciousness, incapable of self-abandonment. Trapped!' she repeated.

It was there, the horror. She was trapped within and without: the house, the sisters, the brother, herself self-accusing. Was there no escape? It must come from within herself, she must use what resources remained to her—get down to it and write her thesis, try for a Ph.D.—something to silence the incessant rattle of her own thoughts. But how could she work in such an atmosphere, those three figures buffeting, squeezing in on her? If only she had had some money of her own she could have found a room somewhere. But the money was theirs, she had nothing. She was beginning to understand now, with the approach of middle-age why they attached so much importance to it: money was freedom. But she was not free; she must be more practical. If he had even told her to go and look for somewhere for them to live . . .

'No, Andrew, I shall not welcome you home. I have waited too long. You are too harassed, you don't have time to concern yourself with such unimportant . . . Unimportant! It was you who could not live with your sisters—you who felt it necessary to go to the extreme of choosing a career which would place continents between you and them! And you think it tiresome of me that I should complain after a winter of no relief from them, where as their guest I am not even a free agent . . . How dare you suggest that it's due to the after-effects of my operation! Do you feel so little for me that you can re-open the wound? Ah, my dear, that knife has two edges . . .' She smiled. She had an ally; she was not alone. Why should she not ingratiate herself with Anthea? It was so simple. Of course they could all live together. How right he had been—it had sorted itself out! There was no need to find somewhere else, no need to reawaken family jealousies about the house. And even she would have her niche—the house in the country. She would have a room there where she could work in peace. She would go down there during the week with Cara and Lucy. Cara would cook and look after the house and Lucy would be kept out of Anthea's clutches. Besides, Anthea would not have time to fuss over a child as she would be too busy looking after her brother.

'Well, my love,' she tore up her husband's letter, 'I'll trouble you no more. As you said, it was ridiculous of me to have made myself a nervous wreck over something so . . .' She dropped the pieces one by one into the waste-paper basket, then ran downstairs calling:

'Anthea! Yoo-hoo!'

She found Anthea in the kitchen berating the servants.

'Oh, it's you!' Anthea turned to her, her face flushed and indignant. 'What are you doing down here?'

'I see it's coffee-time!' Juliet exclaimed brightly. 'Give me the tray, Annie, it will save you a journey.'

'You shouldn't spoil them,' said Anthea as she followed her upstairs to the drawing-room, 'that's not the way to get the best out of them. Oh, dear, how difficult they are at times! One has to be perpetually at their elbow. I know you think that I have very little to do—but you're mistaken there. Believe me, it's no holiday running a house like this!'

'My dear Anthea, you manage beautifully. Why, it's a tribute to your powers of organisation that one is so little aware of any domestic activity taking place.'

'D'you think so? I sometimes wonder . . .'

'I had a letter from Andrew this morning.'

'Oh, yes, I saw you had a letter from Andrew . . . Well? Any news?'

'No, nothing of interest—he said nothing at all really.'

'But his plans?'

'No, nothing further about his plans. He still does not know when he will be coming home.'

'The house? Did he say anything about that? Or perhaps you haven't . . . I've not yet written to him myself about it.'

'Oh, yes, I did write to him about the house and he said he really hadn't time to think about such things. So I am working on the assumption that he would prefer me to take the decision. He's so busy that I feel it's rather a shame to trouble him with domestic arrangements.'

'He left it to you? Oh, dear . . .' Anthea gulped her coffee. 'And what do you . . . There's no need to make up your mind just yet. We've plenty of time it seems and I think for everyone's sake you should consider the advantages . . .'

'Of living here—all of us together? I have considered them. I have made up my mind. I think your plan an excellent one. I may have seemed hesitant to begin with, but it was merely that I had not yet got used to the idea.'

'Juliet!' Anthea reached across to her and squeezed her hand. 'You know, in many ways I've done you an injustice. You always seemed to me a rather cold, frightening person—someone one could not get close to. But how wrong I was! Dear Juliet, I'm so happy—so happy for us all. Now you're really sure, aren't you? I should hate you to feel that I'd pushed you into this.'

'I'm quite sure. As you pointed out, it would solve so many problems. And it was clever of you to have shown me the rooms, going over all the things that need to be done. We'll have to get busy, won't we?'

To Juliet's amusement Anthea for once was speechless.

'You know, Anthea, you're very good to me. I've been letting myself slip recently and it was only a true friend that would have pointed it out. My hair—what a scarecrow! Of course I must do something about it! And you are quite right in suggesting that I don't have enough to do. This actually is a more serious problem than you realise. It's as if I had reached a watershed—maybe it's my operation that makes me feel this the more acutely . . . It's as though I had lost my bearings. I need a new focus, something to aim at. And I was thinking that I would like to embark on some form of study, perhaps take a post-graduate degree. The only trouble is that it is difficult to work and look after a family at the same time. I was thinking that if I could have a room at Cheyncotes . . .'

'But of course you can have a room there. What a splendid idea! I know Andrew will be pleased. He was saying in his last letter how worried he was about you . . .'

'Oh? Does he discuss me?'

'Now then, dear,' Anthea patted her hand, 'once you've got your new interest and Andrew is home, you won't need to distress yourself . . .'

'But I'm not . . .' Juliet checked herself. She forced a smile. 'But are you sure you wouldn't mind? I mean it seems so selfish leaving you here to look after Andrew and the house.'

'Well, I won't pretend that there won't be extra work, but it would make me happy to see you have the opportunity to pursue your interests—it would be a shame when you have got a good mind not to use it. I'm such a stupid, ignorant creature that it is far better that I should be the one who sees to the everyday chores.'

'So kind,' Juliet murmured. 'And now, what about our plans? Shall we start with the furniture or carpets and wall-paper?'

'Carpets and wall-paper first—that's the best way. I don't suppose you'd like to go into town this afternoon?'

'This afternoon!' Juliet agreed. 'Why not? What's to stop us?'

※

'Yes, do come and talk to me,' said Juliet, 'nothing could please me more. I was just preparing myself for one of my long empty bouts of sleeplessness . . . But, come in! Don't just stand there in the doorway! You look distressed—come and tell me all about it.'

'It's no good.' Frances slumped down in a chair, burying her face in her hands. 'It didn't work.'

'I'm mystified. Explain!'

'Cheyncotes—I took him there at the weekend . . .'

'Well, that was prompt! Things are happening quickly these days—important changes all round.'

'Not for me.'

'Oh?'

'No, not a flicker. The whole weekend I was expecting him to pop the question, but he never got round to it, so in the end I had to put it to him myself.'

'What then?'

'He said we were better off as we were, that if we were married we would be taxed jointly. You see, I made the mistake . . . Oh, what a fool I was! Having worked myself up to do it I then got carried away and made a mess of the whole thing. I let him think that the house was mine, and . . . Oh, I don't know— it's the things he says, he goes on so much about money that eventually I ended up by pretending that I had a large private income.'

'But if he's so mercenary . . . Didn't this tempt him?'

'Didn't seem to—at least not enough.'

'Well, I wouldn't be too gloomy. It sounds as if you've made your point. For all you know he may just have wanted time to think it over.'

Frances shook her head. 'Oh, it was too awful—not at all as I'd planned. It was pouring with rain, everything looked miserable and the house was so cold and damp that there was no question of staying there. If only I'd done as you said and let you air the place first . . . But you know how it is—I felt that unless I did it at once I'd never bring myself to . . . And he was so unfeeling about it—he's not like us, he has no eye for that sort of thing, the charm of the place meant nothing to him.'

'Wasn't he interested in the house?'

'Oh, he was interested—but not in the way you would think. He was very interested,' she began to laugh. 'You'll never guess—he wanted to turn it into a hotel! Started making plans right away. I think that was where it went to the bad—when I protested. He was furious with me when I suggested we should live there, wanted to know exactly how much I was worth, said he couldn't possibly afford . . .'

'Maybe it's just as well.'

'What d'you mean?'

'When it's not your house . . .'

'That's not the point. It will be my house.'

'I wouldn't rely on that, if I were you. As I said, it's perhaps as well . . .'

'Hey, what's going on? You're not going to tell me that someone else . . . Does Andrew want it?'

'I don't know what Andrew wants.' Juliet paused to gain time; she must not give herself away now that she, too, had an interest in the house and had become by contagion as grasping as her in-laws. 'In your excitement you have misunderstood me. What I was really trying to say,' she coughed, 'this Howard, he doesn't sound quite . . . Besides, why must you marry?'

'Oh, really! It's all right for you—and even Anthea, at least she *has* been married . . .'

'I'm afraid I fail to see why you should consider the condition quite so desirable. There are plenty of things that a woman can do with her life. One doesn't necessarily need a husband. Would it surprise you to know that there are many married women who might envy you your independence?'

'*You* say that?'

'Yes,' Juliet, seeing her astonishment, smiled. 'I do. Do you find it so odd that I should want a little life of my own?'

'Odd? Very! But then,' Frances shrugged, 'that's your headache. Now to get back to me . . . I'm determined—I even made it my New Year resolution that I should be married before the end of the year!'

'What an astonishing family you are! I am beginning to see that under a superficial dissimilarity you are all really rather alike. Why, you're as persistent as Anthea—no alternatives, no doubts, no digressions, you just press on and on. Don't worry so much—in the end you'll get what you want!'

'How unkind of you to make fun of me!'

'But, my dear Frances, I couldn't be more in earnest. I am quite convinced that if you want to marry you will.'

'But when? how?'

'Well, what about one of your other boy-friends?'

'Oh, no, you don't understand. There are so few men that I could possibly bear. Only Howard, with him I think I could just bring myself to . . . I don't know what the reason is, or why it should be different with him—but, anyway, that's how it is!'

'Rather awkward as he doesn't seem to reciprocate and isn't even tempted . . .'

'Is there anything else? Come on, Juliet, put on the old thinking cap!'

'There's the old-fashioned trap.'

'What d'you mean?' Frances went pale. 'What *do* you mean?'

Juliet smiled.

'What a thing to suggest! What a dirty trick! No, no, I couldn't! And in any case, it would be too risky . . .'

'How lucky you are to be in a position where you can afford risk! You are still on the brink of life. You are still a step ahead of your destiny—it has not yet caught up with you. How fortunate! How enviable! Whereas I have no choice. I have made my bed and on it must lie, and Anthea, one might say that Anthea has dug her grave—in which may she rot . . . But you have the power to meet life on your own terms. You can still act! By one bold action you can make or mar . . . Doesn't that excite you? Have you no sense of adventure?'

'That's all very well, but allowing myself to become pregnant . . .'

'Ah, you're not the brave girl I thought you were! But who am I to blame you, I who have always been such a coward?'

'Hey, not so fast! I haven't said I wouldn't do it.

It was just the shock . . . Time to digest . . . I don't know that there would be anything so bad about it. I mean, tit for tat, it's no worse than him expecting to have an endless affair with me giving nothing in return . . . And I must do something. You're so right—one must act! And it's not as if I hadn't decided—there's no point in making resolutions if one doesn't . . .' She left her chair and sat on the floor, pressing her cheek against Juliet's knee. 'You know there is a pattern in all this that is positively poetic. It's the trick Anthea used—she got the house that way. The house? I hadn't thought of that. Perhaps I'd get that, too, Cheyncotes! After all the question of accommodation would be fairly urgent and it would be only reasonable when it was there, somewhere for us to go.'

❊

'Well, Robert, I'm going to write and tell him all about it—what we've been up to—and you must help me write the letter. How shall I put it to him? He can't very well say, "no", not at this stage. He'd have Juliet to contend with—and she did say that he had left the decision to her.

'Ah! I'm enjoying this,' Anthea finished her late-night tea and pushed the tray aside. 'I've always felt it was self-indulgent of me—old-womanish—making Annie come up all those stairs so late at night. But tonight I've really earned my cup of tea. Why, you wouldn't know me, dear, I've been so efficient! It's amazing what one can get through when one really sets one's mind to it. I never thought I had it in me. And Juliet—she even looks different, ten years younger. I never imagined she had that practical streak. Oh, you should have seen us whisking from shop to shop, not a minute to waste, quite takes my breath away she's so quick—you'd think her life depended on it! You'll hardly believe it, but the children's rooms they're nearly ready and it's only a month ago that we first discussed it all. Painted and carpeted in such pretty colours. You should have seen her organising the workmen! They must have been terrified of her, and I must say even I would not have liked to have crossed swords with her, there was something in her voice, that look in her eye . . .

'But the results are there. All that's left now is for them to come home, climb the stairs and get into bed. And what fun it will be reading bed-time stories to Lucy!

'There's just one thing, Robert, that's been troubling me—Andrew. Does he know? Has she written to him? I'd assumed she had naturally, just took it for granted. But he never seems to mention it in his letters, and I thought this a bit odd. You'd think it odd, wouldn't you? Well, eventually I plucked up the courage to ask her—I hadn't liked to before, you know how she is, touchy and peculiar, I felt I had to be careful, she might have changed her mind . . . Well, as I said, I really felt I would have to ask her—and d'you know what she said? She said, no, she hadn't written to him. She looked so surprised. She said, "No, why should I have written? I've stopped writing to Andrew!"

'And what does that mean? She can't have been serious . . .

'Robert, what *does* that mean?

'There's something I don't like about it. It was a bit

too good to be true. Oh, Robert, if only I'd taken you're advice! I've done it again, my dearest, been too hasty, given in to an impulse. I should have waited, got it all cleared up with Andrew, signed on the dotted line. But it seemed so perfectly above board, she was so enthusiastic, and then it was such a surprise—Juliet of all people! Why, I never imagined that she would want to live with our family. You remember all the things she used to say about us, how she tried to turn Andrew against us, saying how ridiculous we were giving ourselves airs and graces when really we were nothing very much. And what was it she said that made Daddy so angry—how she was marrying into that section of society that one could best describe as the "climb de la climb" . . . I never quite understood what she meant, but Andrew thought it terribly funny and he told Daddy the day they had that dreadful quarrel. Daddy never forgave her, in fact it wasn't long afterwards that he became so ill. Does she realise what she did? I wonder if she carries it on her conscience?

'But all that's past. One mustn't dig up the past—particularly when everything's going so smoothly and we're all going to be so happy together. And she's so excited about it, up there night after night till the small hours, moving the furniture about, endlessly re-arranging things, it's always different in the morning. Actually, between you and me, it's beginning to get on my nerves, it keeps me awake, too, all that bumping about, so restless, there's something creepy about it. What does she find to do up there in the attics? D'you know it's got to the stage that I don't really like to go and look to see what's she's done? It gives me a funny feeling as if one day I might find something horrible.

'Oh, Robert, just listen to me! Now if you were here I'd be much more sensible. Perhaps I should take one of her sleeping pills? It wouldn't do to have two insomniacs in the house. But it's not natural just the same. And all those new clothes she's bought and visits to the hairdresser—she must be spending a fortune! And how does she find the time to fit it all in? The energy she seems to have suddenly—there's something daemonic about it. It's always at night that she dresses up—before she goes upstairs . . .

'I told you about that time I met her in the corridor chanting poetry to herself. "It's Blake," she said, "I don't suppose you've heard of Blake?" So rude! It's the way she says things, the tone of her voice. She said it was the thesis she was going to write, how she'd told me about it, the work that she was going to do all alone in her room at Cheyncotes, grasping me by the wrist reminding me that I'd promised that she could have a room at Cheyncotes. Then she opened a book and said, "Look! read! the Proverbs of Hell. I'm in hell, Anthea . . ."

'Yes, dearest?

'You think I'm being over-imaginative? No, I don't understand much about that sort of thing. I was never much of a reader, I never understood literary people. You think it was just a way of putting it, do you? You think she was trying to be funny? Maybe you're right—she has got a peculiar sense of humour.

'Poor Juliet, it must be dreadful not to be able to sleep at night. Why, recently when I've found it hard to get to sleep—listening to her, all those little noises above my head, I think it's stopped and am just dropping off and it starts again, it makes me feel so jumpy —and lying awake in the dark the hours seem so long, all sorts of gloomy thoughts come into one's head and one gets so worked up about it though in the daytime one would dismiss it all as so much nonsense. It must be terrible to suffer this night after night—no wonder she's a little strange.

'D'you think it was wrong of me, Robert, to have taken away her sleeping pills? She wouldn't give them to me when I asked her for them, so I went upstairs when she was still at breakfast and took them away. Perhaps I shouldn't have done that? I did tell her of course, and she didn't say anything—just smiled, you know the way she smiles! But perhaps I shouldn't be so bossy? D'you suppose she thinks I'm too interfering? Oh, dear, it's so difficult to know what's the right thing to do. I mean, it's such a responsibility—just think of it, if she took too many and I had to ring for an ambulance . . . D'you think she'd do that? If she were the sort of person I understood it would be easier to tell whether it was a real danger. But with Juliet . . . You know I wouldn't put it past her to try and give me a fright, just to get her own back on us . . .

'Yes, you said something . . .

'I shouldn't treat her like a child? Oh, I know, Robert, my dear, I know. But it's so difficult, I'm so used to being like that and at my age it's not easy to change one's habits. I know—I'm clumsy, I shouldn't take advantage of her, as she's a guest here and she is the stranger among us, if it were Andrew, for instance, he'd answer back, but I suppose she feels she can't, I suppose she's frightened we'd tell Andrew. Poor thing, it's not pleasant being the odd one out. But still it can't be helped—she is the stranger, and it's not as if I hadn't tried to make her feel at home, to smooth over the differences between us. And what if I do boss her? It's all for her own good. I seem to have spent my life doing that—trying to help and getting no thanks for it. Only you, my dearest, you recognised my good intentions for what they were. Besides it was something that was forced on me, with Mother dying when we were so young, as the eldest it was only natural that I should have taken her place. It was what Daddy wanted, he said "now you've got to be a mother to your little brother and sister, you've got to try and make it up to them so they don't feel too orphaned". And I have tried! Ever since I was a little girl I used to watch over them and I have always taken such an interest in everything they did, so anxious that they should do well, not make mistakes, and I've always kept a home for them, even when Andrew went abroad saying such bitter things to me, I've kept the house warm for him so that he would have somewhere to return.

'Yes?

'Oh, yes, you're quite right, I am making far too much of an issue out of it. And it's such nonsense—those sleepless nights—I shouldn't be feeling like this, I should be feeling happy, on top of the world, with Andrew coming home and everything going so well, all my dreams are coming true. And it's a good thing Juliet is working on her—what did she call it?—her thesis. Not that I could be expected to understand anything about that, uneducated creature that I am! But Andrew will be pleased. He said he had had such an odd letter from her, he wondered if she was feeling unwell, or had I said anything to upset her . . . How like Andrew—always blaming everything on me! But then how can I escape being what I am if he still looks at me as a sort of mother, the mother always takes the blame. But it's a good thing Juliet has found a new interest, you only have to look at her to see how much she's changed for the better, so much more cheerful and more co-operative, listening to common sense for a change instead of acting the cat that walks by itself.

'There she goes now! I can hear her moving about in her room. Now she's opening the door—oh, dear! No, she's changed her mind, she's back in her own room. How silly of me! Of course that's what she's doing—working, reading, making notes . . . Perhaps she prefers working at night, people like that sometimes do, when there's no one around, no distractions. I suppose she finds it difficult to concentrate during the day with people moving around—and at the moment so much to be done. I suppose at night it's the only time that she gets any peace. No wonder she wants a room of her own at Cheyncotes. What an excellent idea that was, and so touching the poor, dear creature feeling guilty about leaving me to cope with the house here! If only she'd realised how well that suited me! But perhaps she did realise . . .

'She's opened the door again! She's coming along the corridor . . . Oh, Robert, is she going to do it again? She's going to stand outside my door, fidgeting with the handle . . . No! Ssh, I mustn't talk so loud! No, she's gone upstairs—at it again, the same thing night after night after night. She's not working, she can't be!

Oh, Robert, what does it mean?

'You know, Robert, I've always been afraid of Juliet. Even in the old days—it was not that she ever said anything, she was so quiet, so polite and yet it all had an edge to it. She used to look at me in that way of hers, as if she were mocking me, I used to feel she knew something, could see right through me. And now the way she smiles—I hear her laughing to herself sometimes—she has the look of someone who has solved an old, old problem and things at last are going the way she wants them to. I don't know why but there's something about her smile that makes me think she's saying to herself, revenge is sweet, the last laugh is on me!

'Yes, dearest, yes, I can hear you—I know what you're going to say . . .

'But don't say it! I know it all too well myself. My nerves *are* getting the better of me. So don't tell me not to be stupid. I may be being stupid, but I can't help it—this thing has got a hold of me, got under my skin, and there are one or two questions, one or two, you know, my midnight doubts . . . I mean, like her not writing to Andrew any more. You can't just brush that off! There *is* something . . . Oh, Robert!

'He hasn't changed his plans, has he? He's not coming back at all! They've decided to separate and he has told Juliet she can have the house . . .

'No, no, that's too far-fetched . . .

'Something different. Some idea she's put into his head, they've worked it out together. It was just a hoax, saying that she'd stopped writing to him, she's trying to throw me off the scent. They've got it all planned, she and Andrew, they must have. If she hadn't known before what she wanted to do she couldn't have been so quick—carpets laid, curtains hung, everything in place—she was just waiting for the moment so that it looked as if it were my idea. Then when it's all finished Andrew will write to me telling me to go somewhere else, that the house is for him and Juliet. That explains it, her extraordinary laughter—she always hated us and now she's having her revenge.

'What else could it be? She must have known. D'you think that's it? D'you think she knew?

'Ah, my dearest, but how can I ask you, when even you did not know? How could I have told you, you who were so high-minded, so naïve in some ways—if you'll forgive me for saying so? I couldn't have told you, you'd have been too shocked, I'm so bad at expressing myself that I couldn't have explained to you why it was only fair, merely simple, natural justice that I should have had the house. And you'd have been revolted by my methods, you'd have thought me sordid, but again it was only natural, women work in a different way. And how could I have competed against Andrew's intelligence?

'It seemed so simple, so water-tight, nothing could have been proved against me, you can't condemn on the strength of unspoken thoughts. Besides it looked as if the pressure had come from Daddy and the final decision to go abroad leaving us in the house was Andrew's, it had nothing to do with us. Anyway it all just happened like that. It just happened that I was pregnant when the lease of our own house came up, and with Daddy not as young as he was . . . Am I to be blamed that Frances was too flighty, too keen on having a good time to look after the place properly?

Is it to be laid at my door that Daddy missed having his life run smoothly and all his little things attended to? And it wasn't my fault—I certainly would not have wished such a thing on myself—that I was so sick that I needed to be looked after by Annie and Mrs. B. And what if we did stay on afterwards? I was so unwell and weary after the birth, it took me such a long, long time to recover, I couldn't possibly have found the energy to have looked for a new house, just couldn't have coped.

'Andrew was so unsympathetic, he didn't see it that way at all, called me a squatter, said I was perfectly all right, threatened legal action. Such a fuss! I got quite worried about it, he said he'd never speak to us again, sever the connection, that I was stealing his birth-right. But I knew it would all blow over . . . At the time, though, I was quite hurt he was so unpleasant, and I had to keep reminding myself that, in spite of his success, he was very young for his age in many ways and—you know—boys will be boys.

'Besides I never once said, never even suggested, not even to you, my only dear one, that it was you and I who should have had the house. I did think that we might all have lived there together, but they didn't like the idea, Juliet saw to it that that didn't happen. No, it was something quite different. After all, in those days it was Daddy's house and why should he have moved at his age. He was quite prepared to, but I pointed out to him—and Mrs. B agreed with me, after all she should know having worked for him for so many years—that he had got to the stage where he really needed someone to look after him. And what if I did tell him that Juliet wasn't the type who could be bothered with an old man? Because she didn't like him, that was quite obvious, he got so suspicious of her and wasted no time in telling her that he thought she wasn't good enough for his son. Not that you could blame her, that sort of thing would be hard for anyone to swallow. But then you couldn't blame me either. It would have been neglecting my duty as a daughter if I'd left him at the mercy of someone who didn't love him. I just couldn't have stood by and watched my poor father being pushed to one side in his own house like a piece of old lumber.

'So it came from Daddy. It was Daddy who said he wanted me to stay on to look after him, begged me with tears in his eyes, the poor, old man he was so terrified. He said he'd leave the house to Andrew, and he was as true as his word, though I must say when the will was read out it came as quite a shock when I realised that he really had left it to him. When you remember the things that Andrew said at the time, "you'll never die!" just like that, as though his father's death were the only thing that would make him happy . . . Of course he didn't mean it, not really, it was just temper. Poor Andrew, that sort of thing used to send him into such dreadful rages, he used to say he had been cheated, that it was quite unnecessary and needn't have happened, that it was all my fault, and when he was angry he used to look so helpless it made me want to laugh.

'But I had nothing to do with it. It was he who decided to go away. It was all perfectly clean and above board, it just happened, didn't it, Robert? Please, Robert, tell me you believe me! You did believe me, didn't you? I mean, if there had been anything wrong, you would have noticed it, you were always so correct, a man of principle, you wouldn't have let me get away with it. Which proves it was all all right.

'It's only Juliet—Juliet with her woman's mind, you know how jealous women are, how treacherous, never quite straightforward. She insisted she didn't want to live in the house, got quite excited about it, said we were all so materialistic, that such things meant little to her. Well, you know how much of that to believe! As if anyone could honestly mean it . . . Oh, no, no! It was for Andrew's benefit, he was so crazy about her, thought her so unlike the rest of us, she was only saying it to impress him, so that he would think of her as a rarefied creature, too noble for us ordinary mortals. But he was taken in by her—all women lie, it's the way nature made us. Why, I could tell at once the first day he brought her here when he showed her round the house, her eyes opening wider and wider, what admiration! what delight! she had never seen anything so beautiful, had never imagined herself living in a house like this. And Andrew hanging on every word! But I could see it, the way she went into ecstasies over the detail, the proportions, such a large garden and, oh, the fountain, she couldn't get over *that*! She wasn't listening to him, not a word, it was the house she was after. I could see the way she sat in the drawing-room, looking around as though she already owned it. And I thought then—no, my girl, not you!

'But she must have guessed, even then, she was always guarded with me, I could never get anywhere near her, no matter how hard I tried to find out—for Andrew's sake—make her admit. But she never said it, gave nothing away, there was never anything you could pin on her. But she must have been chagrined the way things turned out. All the bluff about preferring freedom, that a beautiful prison was still a prison . . . It was bluff, wasn't it? What a blow it must have been . . . And all these years she's been holding it against me, no wonder Andrew was so bitter, it was her fault, it was she who made him say those things, I can see it now so clearly.

'Robert, Robert! Now I don't like the way you're looking at me . . . You're not to do it, dear. It's not my fault if Juliet thinks I arranged things so that they couldn't live here. You can't hold me accountable for other people's nasty suspicions. And if there has been any misunderstanding the best I can do is to try to make it up to them to show them that all their fears were groundless. After all what could be more generous than the way I'm treating Juliet like a sister, preparing to share my home with her, helping her with all those little domestic problems, those endless decisions about fittings and furniture which must be so wearisome to someone with her academic leanings? And it's not as if I'm offering something new. As you know, my dearest, I had always hoped that we would all live together—one large, happy family. It was what I suggested right at the start when you and I first came here. It always seemed to me the ideal solution. I had it all planned so beautifully years ago—oh, so many long years!—but I never lost sight of it, my plan, I never gave up!'

❧

'Hush, hush, little darling, don't cry! Come to Mummy —Mummy's here, it's all right now, now you're safe in Mummy's arms, there no harm can come to you, don't cry, don't cry . . .

'Oh, that cry!' Juliet covered her ears with her hands.

'No, I didn't do it! No, Mummy wouldn't do that, not hide away, not leave her little one to cry and cry in the dark. Did you think I'd never come back? Did you think you would be left there alone in your agony for ever and ever? What despair! What abysses of terror! Than the new-born babe no damned soul in hell can suffer more . . . "One thought fills immensity," he wrote. But what if that thought, if it were a sensation of utter emptiness, filled only by the echo of one's own piercing screams?

'How could I have done it?' Juliet picked up a teddy bear and rocked it. 'How could I have hidden myself away, severing all comfort from the helpless little animal, the unformed soul whose only consciousness was of anguish unmitigated? Their father comforted them, but it's not the same, not the warmth of a mother's arms, that instinctive *rapport* . . . Now then,' she caressed the teddy, 'there that's better, hush now, it's not so bad, life's not so bad . . .' She laid the toy aside.

'But how foolish I am! how deteriorated! Pretending, re-enacting, a child myself playing at being mother—and to what end? As if I believed that if I were to persist . . . He mentioned that, dealt with that one. What was it? "If the fool would persist in his folly he would become wise." And so—"hear the Voice of the Bard!"—shall I persist?

'Come now, take my hand, one on each side, and Mummy will show you round your new play-room. Look at all the toys that she and Aunt Anthea have bought for you. Look at the rocking horse! Isn't he splendid? What a beautiful saddle all in red leather with brass studs round it, his dappled coat and what a lovely mane and tail to flow in the wind when he gallops over the wild moors with you on his back! He's a present from Aunt Anthea—you must thank her! You must be nice to Aunt Anthea, she's so kind, she was a real mother to her children, she understands the things that delight the heart of a little child.

'And look at the other toys, Panda, Rabbit, Golly and that doll with the golden hair and fluttering eyelids. What shall we call her? Arabella? So many toys . . . Why did I buy so many? I went quite mad . . . I don't suppose they'll even like them. The boys are too old, but maybe Lucy is still at the age . . . Does she still enjoy playing with dolls? I can't remember. I've lost contact . . .' She placed the toys in rows around the walls of the new play-room.

'Ugh!' even now she shuddered. 'How I used to hate it all, the baby-talk, the hideous nursery décor, sentimental bunnies, frisking lambs with roguish grins, gnomes, grotesques, the curiously obscene pink elephant with a waggling trunk . . . I never knew what to do with them, what to say, and yet as the children were so obviously enchanted with them how could I hope to bridge the gap and join them in this world of sugar and cotton wool? How glad I was to have left them to Cara in a room upstairs with the door closed!

'Closed! It was always that, an act of shutting out,

closing a door, my ears, closing my heart . . . It was with relief, always the same each time with each child, with Andrew at each new stage, relief and gratitude—to Cara for taking my place, to Andrew for not reproaching, not resenting, leaving me in peace, alone, reduced and reduced till there was nothing left and in the end I was as isolated as at my beginning—only at the beginning there had been hope.

'But is it so absolute? Before it's too late husband and children will return. Can I not re-do, re-make? Need I be doomed to walk the night wringing from my hands like Lady Macbeth the damned spot? What's done cannot be undone . . . Is there no redress?

'Put away those toys! They're no use to you, your children have outgrown them. Put them away, they belong to the past, those coy and furry objects that delight the heart of a little child. Look to the future, to yourself—the change must come from within—next door, in Lucy's room, there's a mirror there where you can see her, the new Juliet with her careful make-up, her expensive hair-style—Juliet rejuvenated. But when I was young I did not look like that, I was never smart, my hair was always a mess . . . What am I trying to do? The time cannot be reversed, I cannot peel off the years nor start again, so what do I hope for?

'Ah, no, not there, not at your own reflection . . . Look out, beyond the glass barrier where the moon shines so softly on the budding trees, where young shoots are pushing up through the old grass and the whole underground of nature is swelling and toiling with new life. There, look outward—now it is spring! —to other things, other people, Frances within whose body there will soon be . . .

'How could you have suggested such a thing! What serpent whispered in your ear: revenge, do it through the sister, the lovely girl, shame and humiliate . . . Was it envy in its crudest form of her physical grace—her sex appeal? Did you envy that? Do I? I can't remember, I am forgetting it all—everything. It seems so long ago, after Lucy's birth, after the third shock I felt numb and even Andrew didn't seem to want so much, didn't need . . . No, no, I am a poor second to Frances—but happy in that role, happy to contemplate her beauty, through glass to admire. And why should I want to be revenged on Andrew? In that sense he has passed out of my life, it was my own fault . . . So why did I say it? If it happens it will be her own decision, her own action—but even so I cannot absolve myself from complicity. What have I done, I who never had the courage to commit myself one way or the other, for good or ill? Why now in my latter-day emptiness have I become a party to something so degraded?

'But is it so degraded? Leaving aside the seeking for advantage, a husband, property, forgetting the man—men . . . It's the woman—"the nakedness of woman is the work of God"—is there not something which transcends all this? Yes, I am envious! But, no, I don't envy, I welcome! I will welcome Frances' child, will spoil, smother it with affection, give it the love I never gave my own . . . It's not Andrew—I have forgotten Andrew—it's Frances, his feminine "alter", who will carry within herself the hope, no, not the hope, the fact of new life!

'And what will you do? I? Juliet? Will I wait serenely for the return of my husband? But that's laughable! How can I, when he means nothing to me, when he has ceased to exist Ah, if only I could see him as Frances sees him! If only I could long for him, yearn as she . . . If I could love him as he once loved and admired me! Poor Andrew, what a mistake you made! Do you regret it? D'you wish you'd married someone different, someone more like your younger sister?

'Poor Andrew? Oh, yes, poor Andrew, but we're not concerned with him. Poor Juliet—it's better not to be loved than not to love, to know that one cannot love. So where will she go, the shrunken creature? Is she condemned? Must she suffer forever this barren self-reproach? No, that will not be Juliet's way! Juliet will find her haven, away from it all, withdrawn in a quiet room, in a quiet house set in pleasantly undramatic countryside, and there Juliet will become what she has always been, what she always ought to have been—a spinster! It will be with a spinster's ardour that she will study those fruits she dare not touch. In choosing Blake . . . But why not Blake? The choice is felicitous—that prophet of the courage that Juliet so sadly lacks, that proclamation of the sublime, the glory and splendour of life that Juliet has so consistently denied. Alone in her white room she will comment with a spinster's tidy precision on the Road of Excess and that Exuberance which is Beauty. A lost soul herself, she will point out—for the benefit of others—that truth, the only truth, is to be apprehended from the sayings of this unsanctified Messiah. A new morality, that splendid reversal of the Deadly Sins:

> The pride of the peacock is the glory of God
> The lust of the goat is the bounty of God
> The wrath of the lion is the wisdom of God . . .

In her white room, herself blanched, utterly discoloured, Juliet will write a neat little essay. Will she find peace—all alone?

'I am drawn to it. I thought I had no desires. I thought I was trapped because there was nothing I craved which would force me out on a new path, impelling me to scale the walls of my prison. But there is! I see it now, a whiteness, a white calmness, order, clarity . . .

'I must sit down. I feel faint. I must go to bed, go to sleep. I can feel it, the white dove, its feathers caressing, closing my eyelids. What gentleness! How miraculously sudden the reprieve! Is it here, then, the experience of grace, the weightlessness, so unexpected the removal of the burden of sin and guilt? Tonight I shall sleep! My little box will remain unopened, I shall need no drug . . .

'Go on! Hurry before it wears off! Get into bed, you idiot, or it will be as it always was and you'll be doping yourself yet again . . .'

Fearful of losing her new-found tranquillity, Juliet ran down the stairs and along the corridor, her eyes half-closed as if to preserve a state of trance, and it was only when she was within a few feet of her own room that she stopped and remained in the same spot quite motionless with terror, staring at the shape, large, white and dim, that blocked her path.

'I shall scream! I think I am going to scream!' She heard herself say.

Instead it was the shape that screamed, loud, coarse

and vigorous. Then a light was switched on.

'Juliet!' Anthea's voice was now so low it was barely audible. 'I should have known! What are you doing? You haunt the place, prowling through the darkness like an evil spirit . . .' She stepped backwards. 'You look so strange you frighten me!'

'Don't be frightened, little darling! Hush! ssh! Come to Mummy!' Juliet advanced towards her, her arms out-stretched. 'Don't be frightened, Mummy wouldn't leave you to cry all alone in the dark . . .'

'You're mad! No, no! Keep away! Don't touch me!'

'But I want to touch you, Anthea. I want to touch your goodness. You're a good person, Anthea. You did not leave your children to cry in the dark—that infinite abysmal darkness! You comforted . . .'

With a very high, very faint squeak Anthea scurried away to her own room and turned the key in the lock. Juliet followed her and listened. For a while there was no sound, then she heard Anthea getting into bed and a muttering voice:

'I don't like it, Robert! Oh, Robert, I'm so frightened. I can't bear it much longer. She's winning, she's getting what she wanted. She'll drive me out! Oh, Robert, Robert . . .'

'It's no use Anthea,' Juliet whispered through the key-hole, 'you can't talk to the dead—there's no comfort there. You should throw it away, that photograph, throw it into the ponds. That's the place where dead things are submerged, dead babies . . .'

'She can't get in, Robert, I've locked the door. Robert, talk to me, say something so that I don't have to listen to that terrible voice . . .'

'You're stagnant, Anthea, you're like those ponds,

full of dead things, dead rubbish. We're all stagnant, you, I, Frances, all in our different ways—no good can come of it. D'you know what he said about it—hear the Voice!—he said, "expect poison from the standing water".'

'Make her go away, Robert, please Robert . . .'

'Expect poison, Anthea,' her sister-in-law hissed into the key-hole, 'expect poison!'

'Just take no notice? Yes, you're quite right, my dearest, it's the only way. Well, we'll change the subject, shall we, to something more cheerful? As I was telling you earlier this evening, I met in Harrods only yesterday you'll never guess!—our old friend . . .'

Juliet returned to her room, got into bed and lay against the pillows laughing weakly.

'Well, there's no beating her—no penetrating of that thick skin, that dulled sensibility! Anthea, that good person, so homely and well-meaning, who has it within her power to make those she claims to love feel utterly superfluous, to render their lives without meaning or savour, and yet it's all done without a single evil action, not even a word of malice . . . In what lies her strength? Is it in those secret conversations with a piece of printed cardboard, so that she's never alone, never without backing? But, then, don't we all do it? I, myself . . . The limits of normality are so tenuous, to say it inside one's head is all right, to say it aloud is bordering on insanity. But to whom do we address this incessant chatter? Is there no reprieve, no true solitude or peace,' she reached out for her sleeping pills, '"in the heart of light, the silence"?

'But how pathetic it all is! How absurd the human creature with its need for communication—connect or die! How foolish of me to have thought that I could have found a haven, could have dreamed of solitude in a white room, nun-like, ordered, sparse! When in the soul there is no quietness, no order—never! The moment of emptiness is at once filled with fair illusions and fiends most foul, and, silence being intolerable, the clamorous voices start up, seeking communion with the Beyond, with God, with the dead, with one's friends, one's idols, even one's enemies, with one's own conscience . . . It's life that's the trap! Nothing is exempt, no one, not even Blake, the Great Bard . . . Don't cheat! Don't pretend you don't know that Blake conversed with Isaiah.'

❧

'Whatever is the matter?'

'Oh, Juliet!' Frances clung to her knees, weeping. 'I'm quite beside myself! What am I to do?'

'Why, what's happened?'

'What d'you mean?' Frances looked up, angered at the incomprehension of her accomplice. '*It* has happened!'

'Oh!' Vaguely, Juliet stroked her dark, glossy hair, confused and embarrassed by the violence of this sudden physical contact.

'"Oh"? Is that all you can say—"oh"?' Frances let go of her and sat limply at Juliet's feet, pressing a handkerchief to her nose.

'But are you sure? How long ago was it? Can you be quite certain?'

'Pretty sure. I haven't had the results of the final tests yet, but I know,' she looked up into the eyes of her sister-in-law, 'Juliet, I *know*.'

'You could have made a mistake.'

Frances shook her head. 'I've got all the symptoms—I've been feeling terrible. I know *something* has happened to me.'

'Well, I must say you don't look too marvellous.'

'That's comforting! Sweet of you to point it out.'

'Well,' Juliet fidgeted, 'I don't know what you want me to say. Aren't you pleased?'

'Pleased!' Frances got up off the floor and sat down in a chair opposite her.

'I thought this was what you had hoped for . . . Oh, I'm sorry—how obtuse of me! It hasn't worked out?'

Frances stared at her blankly.

'Howard, the boy-friend, he isn't going to . . .'

'Oh, that! Howard? No, there was no trouble there —*that's* all right.' She produced a ring.

'Diamonds? Well, at least he hasn't been mean with you. That's not the sort of ring a man buys if he bears a grudge . . .'

'No, no trouble there, no trouble at all. He even seemed quite pleased, I could hardly believe it. Oh, dear, how peculiar—what a mess it all is!'

'I'm afraid I don't understand. You're marrying the man you wanted, he's not reluctant, doesn't feel he's been tricked, there's nothing unpleasant—and you're going to have a baby!'

'Oh, don't! Don't rub it in!'

'But a month ago you were quite frantic about it, you thought you'd never get married.'

'Yes, yes, don't say it! I've asked for it . . . Oh, it's so difficult to explain! I was so sure that this was what

I wanted—it got right under my skin, I couldn't think about anything else. And yet, now that I've got it, it means nothing to me, I don't want it at all. But I don't suppose you'd understand that sort of thing? You're so much more reasonable . . .'

'Yes,' said Juliet quietly, 'I do understand—very well.'

Frances buried her face in her hands.

'Listen, you mustn't take it like that! It will all work itself out. Besides, there's more to it than getting a husband and the change of status, something much more important—wonderful, mysterious . . . I'm glad.' Juliet gazed at her tenderly, 'It makes me so happy to think that you are going to have a child! You once told me Howard looks like Andrew . . . If your baby is a combination of the pair of you, what an enchanting little creature it will be! You mustn't be so distressed. There's nothing like it, the joy of new life! The winter is over—your winter. Now,' she smiled radiantly, 'it is spring!'

'Oh, my God! What on earth has got into you? That's the sort of drivel one expects to hear from Anthea . . . But you! What makes you think I want this baby? I don't! The whole thing fills me with panic. Yes, panic! That's what I feel—nothing else!'

'Well, what about the—er—forthcoming marriage? I thought you were desperate to get married? What about that resolution you made?'

'But don't you understand? I don't even like him! The man's a cad! If he didn't find me physically attractive and if he hadn't thought I had some money . . . Don't you see? It's that that made him come like a lamb to the slaughter . . . Cheyncotes—that disastrous visit—it made all the difference. He even said so himself!'

'You must have known this before. When you talked about him in the past it was quite obvious. I thought you had no illusions, didn't mind, that there was something else which compensated . . .'

'Sex, looks, it was the sight of him across a room—usually when he was making up to some tarty blonde! Oh, it doesn't matter in a boy-friend, but in a husband . . . And then there's that business about the house. How can I tell him that I have no money, or at least nothing worth mentioning?'

'Poor, old Frances, you have got yourself in a muddle, haven't you? I begin to see . . .'

'Juliet, you've been a good friend to me—I mean, we are friends, aren't we? I know you used to dislike us and that things were difficult for you when you and Andrew first got married, but it was Anthea not me who caused the trouble. You do believe that, don't you?'

'Those days are an epoch away—another world, with different people in it . . . Why d'you bring this up? What d'you want?'

'Andrew—could you make things easier for me?'

'Oh, don't worry about that—he needn't know. You'll be married by the time he comes home.'

'But surely wives always tell their husbands the interesting secrets'

'Not necessarily, not after the first few years . . .'

'But I want you to tell him. I want you to make it all right. He will listen to you, won't he? I mean, at one time he would have done anything you asked him. He wouldn't have listened to any of us, but you —he'd have agreed with anything . . .'

'Was it really like that? It's so long ago—my memory is fading. You forget that it's a long time since you've seen us together.'

'You mean you can't? You don't influence him? You're fobbing me off! You don't want to help me!'

'Oh, for heaven's sake, be reasonable! Of course I'll try and soften the blow, if that's what you want. But I thought it would be simpler if he didn't know, especially when one considers . . . You wouldn't, surely, want him to know *everything*?'

'Oh, you've got it all wrong! That's not what I meant at all. The house—Cheyncotes—couldn't you persuade him . . . Perhaps he might give it to me as a wedding present?'

'You take my breath away! Well, well, well!' Juliet folded her hands, too astonished to comment further.

'I knew you wouldn't do it! But then why should you? Anyway perhaps it wouldn't be in your power—from the way you talk one would think that your marriage was on the rocks. And that, too—it would all be part of the picture. Suddenly everything, but everything has gone wrong.'

'Would it distress you,' Juliet listened to herself astonished, 'would you be upset if Andrew and I were to separate?'

Frances was not listening. Again she had hidden her face and was sobbing, quietly at first then convulsively.

'I don't know what to do! I'm cornered! This is the worst moment of my life . . . Juliet, please, tell me! Tell me how to find a way out!'

'But I don't see what I can do to help you.'

'You must! It's partly your fault. It was you who first put the idea into my head.'

'That's all very well, but you can't blame me for it. It was your action, your responsibility. You didn't have to do it.'

'Oh, I know! I know! All I'm asking for is another idea . . . Help me out, Juliet! Find a way . . .'

'Then if you're certain you don't want to marry him and you don't want the child you'd better have an abortion.'

'An abortion! But what a fiendish . . . How can you suggest such a thing! I couldn't possibly, I'd be too scared . . . I mean, it wouldn't be right—the sacredness of life and all that—one can't tamper with . . . Why the very word sends shivers down my spine! And that you, Andrew's wife, someone I trusted . . .'

'Look, Frances, I'm tired. I don't want to hear any more about this. I'm sorry you're so upset, but it's your problem and you'll have to cope with it yourself.'

'Oh, you're just the same!' Frances' face was flushed and swollen. 'You and Andrew . . . That's the sort of thing he would do—offers help, seems to hold the secret, the sort of person you think you can rely on to help you out of any difficulty—and yet, when it comes to it, he just throws the ball back and leaves you stranded. I thought you—but, no, you're just the same!'

As Juliet listened to her, as she looked into her fine dark eyes, she saw through them the eyes of her husband, through this weak girl the strength of the brother, the real person who she so deceptively resembled. It was as if he were there, in the room, so close that she could smell his skin, hear his laugh, that wonderful laugh, his voice . . .

'How odd that you should have seen Andrew in

me and that I should have seen him in you! How absurd that I should have based my hopes on you, that I should have thought of you as being the one who had it, the real thing—life!'

'What are you saying? What are you talking about?'

'Oh, do cheer up! I was talking about your beauty, my dear. You are a good-looking family—Anthea perhaps not—but you and Andrew . . . You both have it, that physical excellence, creatures made for a better world, that glow . . . Oh, do stop looking so depressed! You won't lose it, you know, many women look their best when pregnant.' As she said this she realised, with a little thrill of malicious pleasure, that Frances would not be one of those women, that the earthy process would drag on her, remove her sheen and she would become ordinary. 'I myself,' she added brightly, 'have never looked so well before or since. You may find it hard to believe but I was really rather pretty when I was expecting. It's a happy time in a woman's life.'

'Then why did you say I should have an abortion?'

'What an exasperating creature you are! You asked me how you could escape having this child. Well, what other way is there?'

'But an abortion . . . Oh, no, I wouldn't dare! And it's not right—you know it's not right! You can't just snap your fingers at it, you can't play with life like that!'

'You? I? I can't?' Juliet began to laugh, her whole body shook with laughter. 'Oh, can't I?'

❦

'So it ends like this. So it took this descent into the

mire, my corruption of his sister, the sister's own cowardice and greed—crack her beautiful shell and, oh, how mean, how commonplace, how unlovely!—it took this to show me the true cause of my unhappiness? But perhaps I wanted to crack her shell, perhaps I scratched at the surface, found a chink to prise it open to see what was inside. And what did I hope to find? Was it Andrew—my foolish rhapsody when I saw her as the one desirable being in this world—was it him really that I was seeking?

'Oh, how confused I am! Juliet, what an odious person you have become! But why pretend? Why gloze it over with sophistries—the sister, the brother, identity, illusion . . . I can't blame Frances, she has always been as she is now, the creature I saw was a vision of my own making, I can't condemn her because the real Frances is something different. But the pain! How it hurt when it became clear to me, that moment when their eyes merged and it was his eyes that I saw.

'And I had thought myself incapable of love, immune to pain! How bored I was when she talked about her longing for that dreadful man when she saw him on the other side of a room with someone else . . . And yet it was that exactly! The marvellous person seen at a distance, worshipped through glass, the creature of a more fortunate and more perfect world, who would never deign, no, who would not even be aware of one's own existence. How vividly it all comes back to me, at Oxford seeing him with other people at a party and becoming quite tongue-tied although he was at the other side of the room and hardly knew my name, possibly had not even seen that I was there. The sound of his laughter in a café, or finding myself in the library a few tables away from him, that sensation, part excitement, part fear and shame at my own meagreness, a creature of the shadows, the half-lights who could never, never walk as he did openly in the sunshine.

'And yet it happened. He married me. Adored me. And the bliss I should have experienced, the realisation of a dream so unattainable I was ashamed of even wishing it, that happiness was quite absent. It was as if I couldn't believe that it had really happened, as if I were still dreaming and had to keep my eyes tightly closed for fear of waking up and finding my life as drab as it had always been. He said I was quite unlike anyone he had ever known, I had opened a door on another world, it was to me that he owed his freedom, his self-respect. I explained it all away, everything, reduced the fact of love to a theory by telling myself that I had merely been an agent in his life, that he was grateful to me because it was through me that he found the strength, the opportunity to free himself from his family.

'Ah, how bitter in early middle-age to find oneself so undeveloped—still suffering from the heart-sickness of the very young—to love and to know that through one's own lack of love one has lost . . . How grotesque that nothing should have changed, that a woman of my age should yearn to re-experience the first awkward kiss!

'I had everything! And now? It's too late now, it's all gone. The children have a new mother. The love Andrew once felt for me he will never again . . . Never? How can one grasp the meaning of that word? It's unimaginable, like death, one's own death.

'All my little plans, spites, snares, intrigues, with Anthea punishing him by means of the house, with Frances punishing him by removing a last ideal, putting a smear on the gay and innocent little sister. And the moment of squeamishness—oh, no, Juliet cannot sink so low, Juliet, of all people, must not so far forget herself, give herself away . . . She will be independent, that little white room, she thinks she has a mind, her intellect will be her future, disembodied, she will retire with dignity . . . And the undignified truth is that now and at all times the only reality is a calf-love for which there can be no future!

'Think no more! Feel that pain no more! There—your pills . . . Do it quickly! Make an end to this pathetic, this absurd . . .

'But the gift of life? One should not abuse it! What if one has always, at all times abused it? No, she's right, one should not play with life . . . And how strange it is that at this moment of anguish so acute, the re-birth, the fountain jet of an emotion I had thought quenched, utterly dried away years ago, so long ago I can hardly remember, how strange it is that the world should suddenly seem so beautiful, the trees beyond the window, moonlight of a cheap, romantic melody . . .

'Quelle misère!'

❧

'Robert, listen! Who is it? Oh, what a terrible sound! Which of them can it be? Juliet? It's not Frances, it must be Juliet. But so loud! so wild! It can't be, she's not like that, she's so controlled—not that terrible sobbing! Oh, the poor soul . . .

'Something must be very wrong. What can it be that should have caused this sudden . . . I know . . . Don't look at me like that, my dearest. I know I should go and comfort her. I know it's wicked to leave the poor thing to cry like that all alone. But I'm frightened, Robert! Robert, you must believe me, I just daren't get up and go and see—everyone's in bed, all the lights are off, she might have left her room and be wandering about, I might meet her in the corridor in the dark before I had time to switch on a light . . . She's so peculiar, she's got worse and worse, sometimes I've thought she was mad. You see why I daren't go? This may be it, maybe she really has gone mad! And yet it doesn't sound like madness . . .

'Oh, how pitiful! I've never heard anything so heart-rending, like a child waking from a nightmare and finding herself alone in the dark . . . If only it would stop!

'There! It's a little quieter now, not so desperate, more normal. Perhaps I was imagining it? Oh, dear, I'm so ashamed of myself. But I'm not going to! I'm not going to go!

'Robert, I just can't bear it. You're stronger than I am, it's all very well for you. No, I can't bear to see you looking at me like that any more. So I'm afraid I'm going to turn your face to the wall. No, no, I couldn't do that to you—I'll put the light out . . . But if I do that I'll be all by myself in the dark with no one to talk to, listening . . .

'I've no other choice. I shall have to take one of her sleeping pills . . .'

So Anthea fell asleep to the sound of distant sobbing and was wakened the following morning by hysterical screams.

'Wake up, damn you! You bloody woman!'

'Frances!'

'Oh, thank God you're awake!' Frances slumped down at the end of the bed. 'I've been shaking and shaking you. I was beginning to think that you, too . . .'

'What on earth is the matter? Good heavens!' Anthea glanced at her watch. 'Just look at the time! Why aren't you at work?'

From the end of the bed Frances stared at her, in her pale face the mouth dark and wide open worked noiselessly.

'You look like a ghost!' Anthea got out of bed and put on her dressing-gown. 'I've never seen you looking so dreadful. I'm going to get the doctor.'

'It's too late . . .'

'What was that?'

'It's not me,' Frances clutched her stomach, convulsed with laughter, 'it's not me who's the ghost!'

'You mean . . .' Anthea rubbed her eyes, shook herself, then with apparent unconcern she went into the adjoining bathroom where she splashed her face with cold water. 'Ah, that's better! Now I feel more awake, more ready to face the world. I had no idea that the effect was so powerful, perhaps it's because I'm not used to it . . . And now, dear,' she returned to the bedroom, but was careful to avoid looking directly at her sister, 'tell me all about it, tell Anthea what the trouble is.'

'You fool!' Frances' voice was unnaturally low. 'Go and see for yourself—in her room . . . But don't ask me to come with you. Anyway I can't,' her voice had sunk even lower. She got up and rushed into the bathroom, 'I'm going to be sick!'

Moving like a somnambulist, Anthea went out of the door, along the corridor and entered Juliet's room where she found her still in bed sleeping peacefully. She held a mirror over her mouth, then touched the cold hand. She looked at the empty bottle of sleeping pills, then left the room, had a bath, dressed herself, rang for the doctor.

When the doctor arrived he found Frances waiting for him on the doorstep, pale and dry-eyed, and Anthea upstairs seated by the corpse of her sister-in-law, weeping tears of genuine regret.

Part II

'Oh, how I do hate funerals! D'you think it was done properly, Robert? So much has happened in the last few days—it seemed so hurried, such a hole in the corner affair. And yet we did the best we could. It wasn't really so bad, a surprising number of people turned up, I had no idea she had so many friends here, all of them so upset and oddly guilty-looking as if they felt they had neglected her. Maybe it was that which made it even gloomier than it would have been in any case, maybe we all felt . . . And then Andrew unable to come at the last moment because he'd got 'flu or something. I do think he might have made the effort, even if he was ill, people don't die of 'flu. If he'd been there it would have made all the difference. And I really needed his support . . . Oh, how selfish of me! As if it matters what I feel! But he should have come for Juliet's sake, if only to say good-bye, end it all properly, if only to show their friends—I don't know what they must have thought. You'd think for himself, to ease his own conscience he would want to show them that there had been nothing wrong. Still, it's Juliet we should be thinking of, not the other people, and I don't suppose it makes any difference to her now . . .

'Death—it hasn't really sunk in, it doesn't mean anything. It was such a shock—I still can't believe that it's really happened. And I don't suppose I ever will believe it—I can believe in anything else, anything at all, but not this, the removal of someone I have known for so long, who has been so much a part of my life, removed so suddenly, neatly, absolutely, as if they had never existed at all. I've buried so many of my dear ones, Daddy, you, my darling Robert, and now Juliet . . . And yet I still don't believe that you're dead, I can't, I won't, it's not possible that you can be nothing . . . How fortunate one is if one can believe in the After-Life! Poor Juliet, if only she had had that comfort—if she had been a church-goer, perhaps she would have found strength, would not have felt so alone . . .

'But it's not true! Frances is wrong about it—it was an accident! What makes Frances so sure that it was —no, I won't say it! It wasn't that, Juliet wouldn't have done a thing like that! What a wicked girl Frances is—it takes a crisis to show people in their true colours —how could she have imagined, how could the thought have even entered her head that Juliet had done it to get her own back on us? What nonsense! As if anyone would throw away their own life just for spite! And it's not as if there had been any reason for it, she had been so excited about Andrew's return, so busy re-arranging the house, we had been getting on so well, doing it all together, I felt as if I was getting to know her for the first time. Though she did change towards the end, all that walking about in the middle of the night, that odd thing she said about not writing to Andrew any more. Was it him? Had he said something, was there more to it than we were aware of? He can be so brusque at times, thoughtless, but then men are like that, a woman would have had more tact . . .

'What shall I say to him, Robert? I must write. I've been putting it off and then I expected to see him when he came over for the funeral. But I can't put it off much longer. I was waiting for him to say something, but there has been nothing, just a cable in reply to mine saying that he would come for the funeral then another that he was unwell, that he regretted, was feeling dreadful about not coming but was sure I would do everything as it ought to be done. And then nothing. Perhaps he's waiting for me, for an explanation. But what is there to explain? I can't tell him that he left her on her own for too long, that wouldn't be fair now that there's nothing he can do about it—even if it is the truth.

'Then what am I to say for my own part? I feel as if I were in some way responsible. I did take the precaution of removing her pills, it did vaguely occur to me that there was a possibility—but I should have known that she would get new pills, it was so stupid of me thinking that I could control it like that, treating her like a child. And then that night—oh, Robert, I should have done as you said, I shouldn't have switched the light out so that I couldn't see your eyes . . . That crying! If I'd gone to her, if I'd tried to comfort, it would never have happened. I could have given her one pill and taken the rest away, stayed with her till I was sure she was asleep. Oh, Robert, what a thing to carry on my conscience! It will be with me till the end of my days! I can't excuse myself. There is no way in which I can talk myself out of this one. It's too clear, too simple—and now the chance of repairing it is removed forever . . .

'Poor Juliet, to think that anyone could have been so unhappy! Even if it was an accident—as I'm certain it was—there must have been something wrong that she was unable to sleep. What made her cry like that? Oh, Robert, I can't forgive myself! I think it's the worst thing I've ever done in my life—or not done. Sometimes it's the things one doesn't do, what do they call it—sins of omission? And poor Andrew. Just think of it, never to see her again and to lose her like that—with that doubt . . . What must be going through his mind?

'You know, Robert, we were wrong. Yes, wrong. No, not you, I can't include you in this, you did not realise, you weren't aware . . . It was me, the guilt rests with me. I've tried to live a good life, really I have, I didn't have the things the others had, their looks, Andrew's brains, I didn't even have their charm, but I have tried to do the right thing, I have—oh, I know it sounds so stuffy!—but I have tried to be a good person. But looking back on it I really can't say I've succeeded. There were so many things that I could have done that I didn't, and I was always so wilful, when I really wanted something there was no stopping me, it didn't matter how long I had to wait or who stood in my way . . .

'You know it's a terrible thing that it should have taken this, the death of poor Juliet, to make me hold up a mirror to myself. And, oh, I'm not pleased, not pleased at all with what I see! Dear Juliet, to think

I was so suspicious of her, right up to the end, and yet she was such a kind, considerate person, such a suitable wife for Andrew. It really breaks my heart to think of all the things I said about her, how I turned Daddy against her—he didn't object to her to begin with, though he was a little disappointed of course—how I tried to make out, and at the time I was convinced of it, that she was marrying Andrew for his money. And all that business about the house—it was me, I knew what I was doing. I knew Andrew wouldn't have the heart to turn us out, I knew that if we stayed long enough—and with Daddy's backing . . . Oh, how sordid it sounds! It wasn't quite like that, not really, not quite so cold-blooded—I mean, I didn't sit down and think it out step by step. It just happened, it could have been accidentally, in a way it was partly by accident, I didn't have to think it out, it just came step by step. But it needn't have happened. If I'd done something, instead of not doing it, doing nothing at all, just staying put so that there was no room for them . . . I know Andrew took it very badly. He took it as meaning something more than just the house, felt that I had taken something away from him that was his right. And poor Juliet, how dreadful it must have been to have married a man who had had to make sacrifices on her account, whose family disapproved of her . . .

'Robert, you had such a high opinion of me, but I didn't deserve it. I'm not, I never was the person you thought me. It's not that I'm trying to exaggerate, I'm not trying to paint myself, appear more colourful, as a black, black sinner. But I've slipped up on many things—and worse, I've been responsible for, neglectful . . . I've thought too much about myself, been too engrossed in my own narrow little life.

'But it's not too late! So long as one lives and breathes it's never too late to make amends. And that now is where my duty must lie. My own life is finished, my personal life, our years of happiness—such happiness!—together are past. So I must forget myself and think of others—of Andrew and Andrew's children. I must try to put right the wrongs of the past. Not that I can ever replace Juliet, a sister can never replace a wife, the mother of his children, and I'm far too stupid to be a companion to him as she must have been. But I can provide a background, I can make a home for them. Poor dear, he will be so lost without a wife—men don't realise how much there is to be done in the way of day to day domestic arrangements till suddenly they have to see it themselves. And Andrew is not any ordinary man in the street. He holds an important position in the world, he won't have time for the mundane details, more than other people he needs to have his life run smoothly, without worries, without all those little problems like the children's clothes, packing their trunks for school . . .

'And the children, what will they do without a mother? That girl they have—no, it's not the same, a stranger doesn't have the same love to give, it's just a job. And if there's one thing I'm confident about it's that. I mayn't have been much good at the other things, I was never clever or talented, I couldn't have taken a job like Frances writing amusing little articles about this and that, I never had their gifts. I'm a simple person created for simple things, the home, family, tea-time and bath-time . . . And now that my own children are growing up I will have all the time in the world to give to my poor niece and nephews. Why, little Lucy—there are so many things that we will be able to do together! I'll take her to the zoo and to the pantomime, that swing in the garden I'll get it mended, I'll get the seat re-painted. Oh, I know I can never fill the place of her mother, but, between you and me, Robert—oh, it's wicked to criticise the dead—but still there's no use pretending, nobody gains by that, and, well, Juliet wasn't what you'd call a really natural mother, I mean, she always expected them to behave like adults even when they were tiny, she didn't have the knack, the right approach. You've got to pretend with children, you've got to make a little magic for them.

'What a blessing it is that I'm here to look after them! Really things couldn't have worked out better what with Andrew being posted to London and . . . Oh, dear, what am I saying? It sounds as if I were glad that poor Juliet . . . Oh, I'm so confused! I didn't mean that—you know, Robert, that that wasn't what I meant! Juliet was such a dear person, the sort of person one appreciates more the more one knows them and by the end I had become very attached to her. I really am sorry—quite apart from the shock and the horror—I really do miss her. Oh, I know we'd had our little differences, but when one looks back on it these things are so unimportant, and one can't help missing someone one's lived with and who has been part of the picture for so long.

'So that reinforces my resolution! I must do it for Juliet's sake. I must make amends for any unpleasantness in the past by dedicating myself to her children, seeing to it that they have all the things she would have liked them to have, giving them the security of a happy home to return to, doing my best to see that they don't suffer too much from the loss of their mother. Why, it's as clear as daylight—my duty is to Juliet's memory!

'And now we shall have to get down to the practical details. I wonder which room Andrew would like? Perhaps he would like this room? Would you mind, Robert, if I gave him our bedroom? It's not, my dearest, that I am being disloyal to you—wherever I go I shall take you with me and will see your dear face beside my bed, I will still be able to talk to you . . . But I feel, if Andrew would like it, he really ought to have this room. It is his house and it's only right that he should have the best bedroom.

'Where the children are concerned there's very little that will have to be done, as poor Juliet saw to all that. How sad it is to think of her working day and night, building a little nest for her babies! I shall write and tell Andrew—not that I haven't told him before—but I'll tell him again all about the preparations she made, how the house is just ready and waiting for their return. And I shall make it quite plain to him that this time there will be no question about it, that it's his house, I shall take second place, he will be the master.

'Of course, now that things have turned out so sadly, we'll be much less crowded, especially as he won't need that girl any more. No, that's one thing I shall insist on. Juliet may have needed her—she had so many other interests, she hadn't the time to devote herself to her children—but with me it's quite different.

Besides, with Annie and Mrs. B here it would be quite absurd and an unnecessary expense to have an extra servant in the house.

'And then Frances . . . Well, things *have* taken an unexpected turn there! What do you think of that, Robert? As if I didn't know what had happened—I wasn't born yesterday! Vomiting night and morning and the day she fainted on the stairs . . . And to have passed it off as the shock of Juliet's death—really that's going a bit far, disgraceful I'd call it, making use of her poor dead sister-in-law to cover up her own sordid . . . Poor Daddy, he'll be turning in his grave! I wonder who it can be? I suppose it's that wretched man she keeps talking to on the telephone—that Howard! Oh, she thinks I know nothing about it—but what does she take me for? Of course I know, I've made it my business to find out, after all it's my responsibility as her elder sister. I've been told all about him, everything, what he does, where he lives, his character, background, and I must say he sounds most unsuitable, just the type one would expect to . . . But then it's her own doing. She's been heading for something like this for years—it's surprising it hasn't happened earlier the way she's carried on.

'Well, the answer certainly is simple. She'll have to get married. She has no alternative. The sooner the better . . . Of course, if it was going to happen, it couldn't have happened at a more appropriate time with Andrew and the children coming home and no place for her here. But what a tragedy that it should happen in this way and with such a man. At least that's one sorrow that poor Juliet will not have to bear . . . If only she were here and could help me to cope, she was so sensible, I'm sure she would have been able to give me some good advice.

'Now I know what you're going to say, dearest, I shouldn't be thinking of her like this . . . But it's not easy carrying it all on my own shoulders, acting as head of the family in this time of trouble. If only Andrew were here!

'But what's going to happen, Robert? She will marry him, won't she? I mean, she couldn't possibly stay here with innocent children in the house . . . How will Andrew take it? D'you suppose I ought to tell him, is it my duty? Or d'you think it would be better if he didn't know, if she just got married quietly and it was all settled and done with by the time he came home? It might be kinder that way, after Juliet, the double shock . . . Besides, if I tell Frances that I won't give her away she might listen to reason. I could put it to her in such a way that she would realise I might tell him, that if she didn't do the sensible thing I would have no option but to ask his advice. She's been so hysterical recently, crying her heart out. She says it's for Juliet, but I don't believe that, not for one minute, it's not all for Juliet. Cheyncotes—she keeps bringing up the subject . . . Well, I don't know why she doesn't come right out into the open with it because I know exactly what she's after! But, no, she'd better stop thinking along those lines, because it's quite out of the question. Cheyncotes also belongs to Andrew, it's his house and he needs it for his children so that they can have somewhere to go during the holidays, the country will be so much healthier for them. And in any case it's all arranged, Juliet and I, between us we . . . Surely she wouldn't want to go against the wishes of her dead sister-in-law?

'No, I shall have to put it to her—even if it's forcing her hand it's for her own good, there have been quite enough quarrels in this family and she wouldn't want to fall out with Andrew—I shall have to say to her in plain English, "Be a sensible girl and Andrew shall know nothing."

'Well, at least there's the baby to look forward to. It's a macabre coincidence that Juliet should have died the moment Frances became pregnant, one person passes away and the gap is filled at once. Remorseless, brutal almost, but I suppose it's nature's way of providing a compensation. But perhaps it's just as well . . . We can't live in the past, with the dead, even I, dearest Robert, can't live only with my memories. Life must go on!'

❧

'Dear Frances,

'Of course I was both very shocked and very distressed by Juliet's death, but I am surprised that you should expect a sentimental lament from me. Anthea perhaps—but not you. As you know I once loved her very much and we have since been reasonably happy together. As I am the person most affected by her death I really don't see why I should be expected to commit my feelings to paper. What do you want me so say? What can I say? Juliet, the woman who was my wife is dead and it's only natural that I should grieve.

'I resent, too, the suggestion in Anthea's last letter that the whole thing was somehow my fault. I don't know whether you share her opinion, but in case you do I should like to clear the matter with you. When someone dies from an over-dose of sleeping tablets and there is some doubt as to whether or not it was an accident, the question inevitably arises as to a motive for suicide. Of course I held myself responsible!

'However, her doctor here tells me that her operation could have made her depressed to the point of imbalance no matter how happy her circumstances. This being the case and as the coroner's verdict was anyway one of accidental death, I intend to absolve myself from guilt towards her, as now that she is dead it is not going to make her suffer less if the rest of my life is blighted by remorse.

'When Anthea had finished with her reproaches, she slipped me the news that you were on the verge of matrimony. She seems keen that you should go ahead, though I gather she considers the lucky man an undesirable character. I'm sorry if the latter is true—not that I have great faith in A's judgement. Nonetheless, even if he is not the only man in the world for you, I feel that if you are attached to him— and Anthea insists you are—you should proceed and take the plunge.

'It's no use, Frances, hanging on me and expecting me to solve all your problems for you. You can't remain the helpless little sister forever. You're in a rut and if you don't get out of it soon you never will. Even if the marriage isn't ideal—and what marriage is?—it is better that you should be *in* life rather than drifting endlessly over the surface.

'So do it and my blessings go with you, don't do it and I'm afraid you will no longer be able to take refuge in the sympathy of Big Brother. I am heartily sick of being a general fairy godmother to you all. My real responsibilities are elsewhere. I have my own children to consider . . .'

'Poor Juliet!' Frances murmured, as she folded up the letter and put it away, 'I doubt if even Howard could have dismissed me quite so cold-bloodedly . . .' But perhaps there was more to it than that, perhaps he really was upset, the only difference between him and another man being that he had had the courage to say openly that remorse after the event was useless.

Remorse after the event . . . She got up and went over to her dressing-table where she stared at herself in the glass. Had it really happened? Was it true that there inside her, forming quietly, growing . . . And then Juliet . . . What was it that had made her so certain that it had not been an accident? Was it—curiously enough it had been the way she had talked about the baby with such delight, rhapsodising about the thrill of new life, the beauty, the wonder . . . That alone had been quite enough of a shock, coming from Juliet it was so out of character that it had made her feel quite peculiar. And then, the very next day, on top of her own private troubles, finding her there that morning . . . Horror upon horror!

She studied her reflection in the glass, but it told her nothing. There was nothing there, nothing to reflect. She felt quite blank. It was not possible that she was going to have a child. She told herself that it would all be all right, what with Howard taking it not too badly and the family raising no objection. She tried to think about the child, be positive about it, but she could feel nothing, no tenderness, not even curiosity—not even fear. It was as if all emotion had been buried with Juliet, her confidante . . . And now, getting the brush-off from Andrew, that really put an end to . . . Everything was at an end, cold and dead!

She got up and left the room to find Anthea. As she walked she was surprised how heavy she felt though she knew she could not possibly at this stage attribute it to her pregnancy.

Anthea was in the drawing-room looking through an album of photographs. 'I was just sorting these out,' she explained as Frances entered the room, 'the ones of Juliet—I thought Andrew might like to have them.' She fumbled for a handkerchief and dabbed her eyes. 'Oh, dear, how happy she looked—those photographs of them together when they were still at Oxford. I wonder if I should send them to him? D'you think it would merely make him more upset than ever? No, on second thoughts I will send them—he really ought to have them.'

'Why? Are you so anxious to get rid of them?'

'Now then, Frances! No, I think it would be nice for him. I'll send him the happy ones. It will be nice for him to remember that they had been so happy, that there once was a time . . . Poor Andrew, how he must be reproaching himself!'

'I thought you thought it was an accident?'

'I don't think, I *know* it was an accident. She was in the habit of taking too many. When the first lot didn't send her to sleep she would take some more and then she couldn't remember just how many she had taken. I knew this happened . . . Oh, if only I'd watched her more carefully! Poor Juliet—when it was all so unnecessary!'

'Well, if it was an accident, why should Andrew feel guilty about it?'

'No, dear, you don't quite understand.' Anthea pursed her lips. 'It was the fact that she needed to take those pills at all . . .'

'But she was always like that, she'd been an insomniac for years!'

Anthea sighed, applied her handkerchief to her eyes and returned to the photographs.

'By the way, Anthea, I've got a bone to pick with you.'

'Yes?' Anthea sniffed through her handkerchief. 'Have you?'

'What did you mean by telling Andrew I was about to get married?'

'Well, you are, aren't you?'

'Maybe, maybe not,' Frances shrugged. 'But that's not really what I was trying to get at. What I want to know is why you told him you were so keen I should get married to someone you thought was a pretty beastly person?'

'What was that, dear? I'm afraid I don't follow you. What are you trying to say?'

'You heard me. You know perfectly well what I was saying!'

'My poor Frances,' Anthea shook her head.

'Poor Frances, be damned! What makes you think I'm so in need of your pity?'

'Now, dear, don't get so excited! I know you're over-wrought—we're all feeling a little tense, still suffering from the after-effects. But you needn't use that tone with me—after all I am your sister. I'm not accusing, I'm not going to lecture you.'

'But about what? Why should you lecture me?'

'Don't be tiresome, dear, it's happened and there's no point now in wishing that it hadn't, there's nothing you can do to undo it. In the past perhaps, if I'd pointed out the possible consequences of your way of life. I see now I neglected my duty to you, I should have taken a firmer line . . . But then who was I to meddle with you—you always made out that you were perfectly happy, that you got much more fun out of life than a homely old body like me. It was not as if you were still a child.'

'So you know . . .'

'Frances, dear,' Anthea took her hand, 'he will marry you, won't he?'

'Did you tell him?'

'Him?'

'Andrew.'

'Oh, him! No, I didn't tell him. I didn't want there to be even more unpleasantness—there has been quite enough already. Besides, while I as a woman can sympathise, he mightn't look at it in quite the same light. And, for his sake, too, after the shock of Juliet . . .'

'Are you sure?' Frances looked at her suspiciously. 'Oh, I suppose you can't have told him. He'd have said something about it. He never was the type to gloze over the things that are unpalatable. He doesn't waste time by pretending, never bothered to lie either to other people or to himself. It was something I used to admire in him. But—oh, I don't know—that sort of thing can be taken too far . . .'

'What's the matter, dear? Has he said something that's upset you?'

'He also thinks I should marry. You're both pushing

me into it!'

'But I don't understand. I don't see what the objection . . .'

'You don't? And it was you who told him that Howard wasn't a particularly nice person. That's what gets me! I can't understand how you could be so mean as to push me into marriage with someone with whom I would probably be unhappy.'

'But you've no alternative. You must marry, and if he's the father . . .'

'Anyway how do you know all this about him? I'm not saying you're not right—alas, you are! But how d'you know? You've never met him.'

'I made some enquiries. Now don't think I was spying on you—I was only trying to help. And I do want to help, you must believe me . . .'

'Then what am I to do? I can't marry someone like that, I can't spend the rest of my life . . .'

'You must. There's not just you, you'll have your child to think of.'

'Why must I? I wouldn't be the first girl who brought up a child on her own. There isn't the same slur nowadays,' she began to laugh, 'it's even becoming quite fashionable—rather *with it*!'

'You can't possibly be serious! I mean, where would you go? You couldn't stay on here, not with Andrew coming home, not with children in the house! It wouldn't do at all! You know that—I hardly need to point it out to you.'

'So you wouldn't have me? You'd turn me out?'

'I'm going to ring for Annie so that she can make us a cup of tea. Your nerves are bad. You need something soothing.'

'It's not tea I need!' Better gin, she told herself, should she try that? 'So this is the plan, is it? Andrew living here and . . . But where will you go?'

'What happens to me is of secondary importance. I expect that between us Andrew and I will arrange something . . .'

'Oh, you don't have to tell me! I know what's going through your head. Once you've got rid of me you'll stay on here with him after he comes back. You'll have the perfect excuse now that there's no one to look after his children!'

'The poor little darlings,' Anthea's eyes moistened, 'poor little orphans.'

'You sicken me! Oh, well, so much for family ties, blood being thicker than water and all that! It doesn't amount to much, does it? It strikes me that no one in this family gives a damn about any of the others—they're all just out for themselves.'

'But you will have a home to go to. And think what you've got to look forward to. Aren't you excited about it—the baby? You don't know how lucky you are. Look at me—all that's over for me, I shall never have any more babies.'

'Please! Oh, you make me feel quite creepy saying that, you remind me of Juliet. I suppose that was what was going through her mind, perhaps that explains it . . . Anyway, to return to the subject, if you have any feelings for me at all then don't push that one, don't talk to me about babies, don't goo-goo at me. If I must marry, I must. But don't pretend, don't wrap it all up in some phoney . . .'

'So you will marry him? Ah, I knew you'd see sense. I didn't really believe . . .'

'As I was saying we're all out for ourselves. Go on, admit it, and it will make the whole thing much more easier to manipulate. Well, the bald facts are that you want to stay on here with Andrew—and, being you, I daresay you'll manage it. I wonder what he'll say? What a laugh! Oh, well, it will serve him right! So, seeing as that gets you fixed up to your own satisfaction, let's concentrate on me and where I'm to live. Now it had occurred to me—I mean we've had such difficulty finding a new tenant for Cheyncotes . . .'

'Cheyncotes?' Anthea started and a couple of photographs fell from her knee to the floor. 'Oh, dear, that brings it all back to me—we'd made such plans, Juliet and I. We'd got it all arranged . . .'

'You arranged with . . . Am I hearing right? You did say Juliet?'

'Oh, yes, she was to have had a little flat there so that she could work in peace—she had decided to take something up, you know, something academic, I was never quite sure what. But anyway she was to have worked down there—it's so peaceful right in the heart of the country—and Andrew could have joined her at weekends and we were all to have spent the school holidays together—at Cheyncotes. The poor thing was so thrilled about it, having a room of her own, somewhere she could concentrate without being disturbed— it seemed to make all the difference to her, she seemed to be taking a new lease of life . . . Oh, Juliet! Why did this have to happen to you?' She bent down to retrieve the fallen photographs, her hand searching blindly as her eyes were now over-flowing with tears. 'So we won't talk about it, not for the moment, Frances, if you don't mind. I really can't take any more. Just don't mention Cheyncotes . . .'

❧

'Well, Robert, I really don't think I care much for weddings either! Why, this was hardly more cheerful than the—oh, you know what I mean—the other ceremony. Oh, dear, what a year it's been!

'Still at least she's done it. We have got that to be thankful for! But you know, dearest, I was beginning to wonder if she ever would. What on earth can have possessed her, waiting for so long—it must be about four months now, I keep getting my dates muddled—till it was so obvious that all the world could see? I was getting really worried, there was a moment when I thought history might be going to repeat itself and she'd just stay on as—well, you know what I'm referring to!

'But what a wretched do it was! I must admit—though it's tragic to have to look at it this way—that that was something you have been spared, I really was almost glad that you weren't here to witness it. Oh, what am I saying? But I am glad, truly glad that Daddy wasn't alive to see it. That dingy registry office and no flowers, no one there except me and that woman he'd brought along . . . Well, I don't know what you'd have said to that! Half-way through I began to wonder if she wasn't—well—if she hadn't been an old friend. D'you think that's why Frances looked so down in the dumps? She's certainly not carrying her pregnancy very well, I don't think I've ever seen her looking so plain, I wouldn't have thought it possible, she was always so immaculate, so conscious of her appearance,

I'd never have imagined if I hadn't seen it with my own eyes that she could let herself go so completely. She just hadn't tried, even her clothes they looked as if they had been put on any old how and it's not as if she's that far advanced, she could at least have tried to hide it instead of standing there so that you couldn't help looking at her profile, she almost seemed to be doing it on purpose . . .

'I suppose *he* didn't look so bad. I feel I must hand it to him that he did appear to be trying to make the best of the sorry business. He's rather handsome really, especially when you see him at a distance, it's only when you look closer that there's something coarse— oh, I don't know how to describe it—but not, certainly not a gentleman. And his manners . . . Maybe it's just that I'm not used to that sort of thing, but I really thought it was going a bit far, giving me *such* a kiss and then calling me "old girl"! Still perhaps he was nervous of me, perhaps he felt he's got to try and cheer up the whole gloomy procedure, and having gone so far didn't quite know where to stop. But there's no getting away from it, it was offensive, almost as if he had had some sort of grudge against me, as if he enjoyed being rude.

'Then the party afterwards—I didn't need to have it said to me, that did make me feel old. What an extraordinary collection of people—I'd never realised that Frances moved in such circles. It was quite an eye-opener! They all looked as if they had been drinking the champagne for hours before we arrived, and I don't know what it was about them but they seemed so immoral, gave me the impression that there wasn't an honest man or woman among them. And the way they joked about Frances' condition—quite shameless—I could scarcely believe my ears! I can tell you, my dearest, that I could hardly wait to get away from them—the smoke, the noise! Oh, dear, poor Frances...

'Well, to look on the bright side, it was at least a nice day—though good weather hardly compensates, and it wasn't as if the circumstances alone weren't bad enough. But there was nothing left but to console oneself with the sunshine and all that lovely blossom outside the registry office and the birds singing . . . But just think of it—waiting until May! And they do say that May weddings are unlucky . . .

'Well, it *is* nice to be home again, away from all those dreadful people. Quite a nightmare really—I'll just have to shut my eyes and pretend it hasn't happened. Not that that's too difficult here, it's so peaceful. And wasn't that kind of Annie to have brought me a cup of tea as soon as I got back, almost as if she'd guessed how much I would need it? And it does help—so refreshing—I'm beginning to feel much better now, more my old self again. There is this to be said for that sort of experience that it does make one appreciate other things. Why, this house, the garden seem like a paradise! Oh, if only you could see it, Robert, here, too, the garden is full of blossom, if only you could listen to the birds, smell the sweet scents that come floating in through the window . . .

'How odd it is . . . Do you realise that this is the first time I have lived in the house by myself. Not that I am quite on my own, I am never really on my own, not with you beside me, your spirit, your influence. But it's the first time there has been no other member of the family. I suppose the house ought to feel empty, but it doesn't, it's so full of memories, shadows that linger . . . Besides, it will soon be full of people, occupied as it ought to be by a large family, echoing with children's laughter—five children, just think of that, all the little cousins!

'And now, Robert, I must ask you what you think of your new surroundings? This is the first night, our first night in our new room. It's quite pleasant, isn't it? I mean, apart from not having a bathroom attached, there isn't such a difference. And a lovely view over the Heath! What a pity you can't see it, now in this early summer evening it all looks so perfect, a pale pink haze over the city and the Surrey hills pale, pale blue in the distance.

'I suppose I might as well enjoy it while it lasts. Soon I won't be able to indulge myself like this, I won't be able to sit back and relax, there's so much to be done. First our old bedroom, Andrew's room, it had better be re-decorated, it hasn't been done for years, not since before you died, I didn't like to change anything. But we'll need to get it done for Andrew, it would be only right, the master returning to his house, we'll need to get everything spick and span for him. And now that Frances has gone . . . I think my original plan was a good one, don't you? I don't see why I should change it, her room would be so suitable as a study. Then the children—well, all that's been seen to. The only thing that remains—and this is a real headache!—is what are we to do with Juliet's room? It's quite a nice room, it would be a pity to waste it. But, oh, dear, *who* is going to want to sleep there? Even now I don't like to go into it, even Annie and Mrs. B—it hasn't been cleaned, hasn't been entered since . . .

'Yes, dear?

'But that's a brilliant idea! Why didn't I think of it before? That wretched girl—if he insists on keeping her, and he seems quite adamant about it, though I don't know why, I just don't understand that one at all, you'd think he didn't trust me with my own niece and nephews. But anyway, as he insists—well, why not? It's not as if she would feel it, would be troubled by the associations, it's not as if she was a relative . . .

'Well, that solves that one. It's all going very nicely, everything is just going to fit in . . .

'What was that?

'Frances? Oh, you don't think I'd listen to her, do you? You don't think I'd take any notice . . . Why, I have it all down in black and white, he said it himself that, yes, I had been quite right when I had pointed out that it was his house and it was time he lived in it, he's well aware of the fact, it is his house and he does intend living in it. Well, what could be plainer than that?

'You were saying? You wanted to add something?

'Oh, that! You mean the other part of the letter? You mean the bit where he said I was to go, that he wouldn't contemplate living under the same roof with me no matter what the circumstances, that he'll give me Cheyncotes and if I don't want to live there I can have what income it brings in, that not to put too fine a point on it he's prepared to pay a high price —very high when you think of it!—in order to keep me away.

'Well, well, well! Saying all that rigmarole it's made me quite out of breath!

'What do I think of that?

'Well, honestly, Robert, what d'you think I'd think? You don't honestly believe that I'd take any notice? Why, I didn't take in one word! Andrew's always been like that—that's Andrew all over! Oh, no, he'll find it's not quite so simple, he can't get rid of me as easily as that!

'Those things Frances said?

'But then you know Frances—she's always been hand in glove with him! But what can she do? She's well out of the way now, hasn't a leg to stand on! And in any case she'll soon be so busy with her own life she won't have time to . . . Poor Frances, I must say I feel quite sorry for her, she won't know herself, she has no idea, not the faintest conception how much work is involved with a new baby.

'Still to get back to what you were asking—those things she said. How I was making a fool of myself, how she couldn't believe anyone could be so blind, could persist in the face of . . . She got quite nasty about it. Really, if I hadn't been able to put it down to her condition—some women do go rather peculiar—and if I hadn't felt so sorry for her and so worried in case she let things drift until it was too late . . . As I was saying, if it hadn't been for that, I would have been very angry. And she put it so bluntly—I suppose it's the influence of that dreadful man . . . Oh, dear, how sad it is to see one's own sister so coarsened, going downhill so quickly.

'Dearest?

'You think I'm trying to pretend she didn't say it? Oh, no! There you're mistaken! Your old Anthea is tougher than she might appear. No, it's not that. It's just that I didn't want to talk about it in front of you—I thought you might find the subject painful, because, after all, you were with me, you were a party to it, even if you weren't fully aware . . .

'Well, as you ask, she said, you don't imagine he doesn't know your tricks by now, you won't manage it this time, you don't suppose you can do it again just by squatting here?

'You know, Robert, now that I've said it it doesn't sound as bad as I'd first thought, nothing of real importance, just the sort of stupid malice that is only natural between sisters, the sort of thing that is said but not meant, and the poor girl, her own circumstances were so trying it's not surprising she wanted to take it out of someone. No, I mustn't be too hard on her.

'Oh, yes, I know she showed me letters she'd had from him and he wrote to me saying exactly the same thing. But I don't believe it. I flatly refuse to take a word of it seriously. I'll have to hear it from him in person, he'll have to threaten me, do his worst, the very worst, remove me by force if necessary . . .

'But it won't come to that. He may think those things now when he's thousands of miles away, but he doesn't see the situation as it really is. There are his children and then there's a home to be run, a house to be kept up. Once he's faced with these things himself he'll be quite glad of someone competent to deal with them for him, someone who knows it all backwards.

'I mustn't?

'Oh, no, dearest, I was only joking! Of course I didn't mean it—you didn't take me seriously did you?

—of course I was only joking when I said he would have to remove me by force! No, no, no, I'm not as bad as all that! Besides, he's my own brother, my only brother, I couldn't treat him—or anyone—like that. No, all I was saying is that he may change his mind. After all, it must have been such a terrible shock for him Juliet dying so suddenly, it wouldn't be at all surprising if it temporarily affected his judgement. So, what I'm going to do is this. I shall stay here till he does come back, have everything ready for him so that he can see for himself how well it would work, and then . . . Well, if he still wants me to go—not that I think he will, not when he sees . . . But, if he does, then there will have been no harm in my staying on, I'll have kept the house warm for him, he'll have everything made easy, it must be so dreadful when you come home from another country to have to get down to all those tiresome domestic chores, getting a house habitable, finding suitable help. Oh, no, he'll be spared all that!

'The other thing Frances said—Cheyncotes?

'But Andrew wouldn't do that! He wouldn't suddenly become spiteful, turning me out of this house and not giving me anywhere else to go. Poor Frances, she's simple in some ways, though she was supposed to be so efficient. Andrew wouldn't do that—it's not in character, he's too soft-hearted basically in spite of the things he says. And in any case he wouldn't dare . . .

'Now Cheyncotes, that was a near one! Frances was so determined . . .

'What, dearest? Frances isn't my sister for nothing! Well, what a thing to say—that's very naughty of you!

'Still it all worked out in the end. I wonder if it was that that made her hang on for so long? But fancy her saying it, coming out with it so bluntly just like that, telling Andrew that the man wouldn't marry her unless he gave her the house! D'you think it was true? No, what nonsense, it can't have been! Luckily Andrew didn't fall for it, though it took him to convince her that he wouldn't part with the place, she wouldn't listen to me. But my heart bled for her, really it did! How she cried when he told her that he was giving Cheyncotes to me! And it did seem a little unfair, as it's not as if I even want it, the idea had never entered my head. But there it is, and as Andrew says it's better that the man should be the provider, it's a bad thing when it's the woman who has got the money, particularly when it's started on the wrong foot in any case. Though he doesn't know that, not unless she's told him herself. I kept my promise— at least I don't have that on my conscience.

'Actually now that we're on the subject of Cheyncotes, I suppose I'd better go down there and see what sort of state it's in. Yes, I can see that it's there that I'll be spending my time. Once Andrew's room is done up and his study and poor Juliet's old room aired and tidied—I might put new curtains in, just something to make it not look too much as it was—well, once that's finished there will be very little to do here. But Cheyncotes, that's another matter! I imagine it will need to be re-decorated from cellar to roof, the mere idea of it makes me feel quite exhausted before I even start. Oh, well I mustn't complain—life's so much more cheerful when one has plenty to fill the days! And what fun it will be . . . I know what I'll do, I'll set myself a target, I'll have it ready before the beginning of the summer holidays. And won't that be a surprise for them—they're bound to be home before then—won't it be lovely all the children, the five cousins, all together in the country for months on end at the very height of the summer?'

❖

Andrew and his family were not home by midsummer, although the house was ready for them and all that remained to be done was to put flowers in the rooms and sheets on the beds. By July even Cheyncotes was habitable and Anthea spent the summer holidays there with her two children. That summer the weather was particularly fine and the children enjoyed living in the country; even Anthea was surprised at the amount of time she spent busying herself in the garden. However, the summer had passed and it was not until early October when her children were already back at school that the great day arrived. It was a gentle autumn afternoon with the trees already golden but not yet shorn of their leaves, and, as she waited on the steps below the classical façade ready to open her arms in welcome, she was pleased to observe that at that moment the house was looking its very best.

A young woman descended from the taxi followed by a little girl wearing a fur hat and muff and her two brothers. How quaint and old-fashioned they look! thought Anthea. It was these continentals, they had such a tendency to fuss and over-dress their children. Oh, well, she would soon put a stop to that! She was surprised to see the nanny—she had decided that she would address her as 'nanny'—open her purse and pay the taxi-driver.

'But where's Andrew—Mr. Haslett?' she called out to her.

'Andrew? Did he not tell you?' The voice was soft, the foreign accent not unpleasant. 'He has some business to attend to. He will be here in two or three days' time.'

Anthea descended the steps and embraced the children; then when she turned to their nanny there was a moment of embarrassment, it was almost as if she, too, had expected to be welcomed with a kiss.

'How do you do, Miss Monti?' she held out her hand to her.

The girl, who seemed to be having some difficulty in removing her glove, coloured slightly.

'I have heard so much about you,' Anthea glanced at the children and lowered her voice, 'poor Mrs. Haslett always spoke so highly of you.'

'Did she?' Her flush deepened. She was a pretty young woman with a shapely figure and dark, gentle eyes. Anthea was surprised to see that she dressed with such good taste. She was surprised, too, by a resemblance to Frances, although, while she was not as striking as her sister, there was something in her manner which suggested a more amenable temperament. It would be all right, Anthea decided, she would fit in, there would be no trouble from this quarter.

'My goodness, James and Stephen, what big boys you've grown into! You'll be able to help Annie with the luggage.' The boys responded obediently and, taking her niece by the hand, Anthea led them up the steps into the house. 'What's that you've got? A muff is it? That's a funny thing for a little girl to be wearing.' The child lowered her eyes and clutched her muff more securely. 'Thank you, Stephen, you've brought in all the cases, have you? Well, now, I'm going to take the three of you upstairs to show you your bedrooms and the new play-room that's just been done up for you—at least it was done some time ago, we thought you'd be home sooner. Oh, Annie, you'll remember to show Miss Monti to her room, won't you?'

Anthea took the children upstairs and after showing them everything that was of interest and giving Lucy a ride on the rocking-horse, she told them to wash and come down to the drawing-room where they would all have tea together.

She waited for them for some time, but instead it was the nanny who first entered the room.

'Oh, it's you! Where are they? They can't still be washing themselves.'

'They're in the play-room. I told them to wait till I called them.'

'Oh, dear!' Anthea pursed her lips. This was a bad start. 'But I told them to come down just as soon as they were ready. Oh, well . . . It's the first day. We'll forget about it this time. And now, how do you like your tea? You do take tea, don't you?'

'Very weak, please. I drink it without milk or sugar —with nothing.'

'Well, I suppose you wanted to talk to me about the children? Now before we start I feel there is something I must say to you—their clothes. Children need plenty of freedom, they don't like wearing fussy clothes, and those little boots Lucy was wearing—oh,

I know they look very sweet on her—but they're not good for the feet, one has to be so careful with children's feet, the growing bones can so easily become deformed. I don't know if you have such things in America, but here one can buy the most excellent children's shoes which are nice and broad and won't cramp their toes.'

Anthea waited for a response, but for a while her companion merely sipped her tea in silence. Eventually she said, 'This is a very beautiful house. They often talked about it, the lovely home they had in England.'

'Ah, yes, that was most unfortunate. After my father died he left the house to Mr. Haslett, but by that time he had taken a job abroad and so he has never really had the pleasure of it. But I am so glad he is coming home now. I have a feeling that he always wanted to live in this house—it meant a great deal to him.'

'Yes, I think so. I think he has always wanted to live here.'

'Oh, if only it hadn't happened that way! If only he hadn't chosen a career that sent him all over the world!'

'He told me there is a fountain in the garden. He said it was one of the things he liked best. He was telling the children and they were so excited.'

'Oh, dear, the fountain . . . How remiss of me! I should have got it repaired. You know, I've been meaning to for years now, but somehow I just never got round to it. It got cracked with the frost during the hard winter after my poor, dear Robert died, and I don't know . . . I suppose I just let things drift.'

'Oh, yes, I can understand . . .'

'Can you, dear? That is very sweet of you . . . You know, I think you and I, we'll get on very well together.'

'But now that there is so much changed,' she paused, then her face shone with sudden happiness, 'now, the fountain, we can get it mended!'

'Oh, but I should have done it myself! I wanted to have everything ready—you know, a real welcome home! I don't know why I forgot the fountain. I suppose I'd got so used to it being like that, it just never entered my head.'

'I liked so much that there was a fountain. In my own country there is so many ornament—it is natural to us. We Italians have such a love of beauty—I don't think it is quite the same for people in other countries —but for us it is necessary to adorn, we like to celebrate, to dress up, yes,' she smiled, 'even our children.'

'Oh? I see! Well, you're not in Italy now . . . Still you can go there for holidays. I expect you'll be glad they've returned to Europe? Do you miss your country, being so far from home? It must be so sad for you being separated from your own people. Still, perhaps you'll tire of living in England, perhaps one day you will suddenly decide to pack your bags and leave us?'

'Oh, no! No, that couldn't be . . . But holidays, yes— how I look forward to it! And you must go there, too. Have you ever been to my part of the country? It is very beautiful, on the shores of Lake Como not too far from Switzerland and the mountains. Ah, how I love the mountains! It must be in my blood, I am Swiss by birth, you see, though I have always lived in Italy and speak of myself as Italian—but I think

I prefer to be Swiss.'

'Do you? Yes, the Swiss are so much cleaner. I went to Switzerland years ago with my father, but I've never been to the Italian lakes. My brother was very fond of that part of the world, he and Mrs. Haslett went there for their honeymoon . . . Oh, dear, I don't suppose he'll ever want to go there again, the memories would be too painful. But I must say it is something I would have liked to have seen myself, I believe that the lakes are very beautiful. But I doubt if I shall go now—it's such years since I have ever been anywhere. I've become so dull, I just wouldn't have the energy to try anything new. It becomes a habit, you know, if you stay in the same spot for too long it becomes almost impossible to move, to do anything about it. Why, would you believe it, there are times when for days on end I hardly stir out of this house? I seem to have everything, here and in the garden—not that I do much gardening, it was only at Cheyncotes this last summer that I actually bothered to get down to it. You see, my needs are so simple that there is really very little that can tempt me out of the house. Besides I'm happy here, I'm so attached to the place, I feel it's become part of me.'

There was a silence. The silence became prolonged and again a flush animated the girl's pale cheeks.

'What a lovely day it is!' Anthea said at last. 'D'you know it was on a day like this a year ago almost exactly that poor, dear Mrs. Haslett first came to this house? She had just come out of hospital after her operation and she looked very frail—but so brave! Oh, if only she hadn't had to have that done to her! I'm sure it was that that was the start . . .' She searched for a handkerchief. 'Forgive me, my dear, I know I should be able to control myself by now, but I can't help being emotional about it, sometimes it just comes over me . . . But poor Mr. Haslett, how terrible it must have been for him! I really must get myself more under control before he returns, it wouldn't be fair, would it, to add my sadness to his? Perhaps it was a good thing that you came on ahead of him, it gives me a day or two to get adjusted—also you can put me in the picture as to how things stand. Tell me, my dear, was he most dreadfully upset?'

'Andrew? Oh . . . Yes, he was, but that is natural, do you not think? It was a great shock.'

'You call him Andrew? Yes, I heard you calling him that before . . . I suppose in America these things must be much more informal. Oh, dear, I'm so behind the times! I find it so difficult to get used to . . . But tell me, if you call him Andrew, what am I to call you?'

'Why, Cara!'

'I see—Miss Monti, Cara . . .'

'Oh, no! I am not Miss Monti!'

'Really? Well, I must have made a mistake, but I was sure Andrew . . .'

'Ah, yes, a mistake! Then he did not tell you?'

Anthea looked at her vacantly.

'But I do not know what to say! It is strange . . . I do not understand that he did not tell you. You see, last week we were married.'

'You got married? So you are Mrs.—what is your married name?' Anthea blinked at her. 'You don't mean that . . .'

'Yes, you and I we are sisters.'

'Oh!' Anthea's cup and saucer fell with a clatter

to the floor. 'Tst! what a mess, how clumsy of me!' She bent down and rubbed the stain with her handkerchief. 'And tea is one of the very worst—I don't know why it should be so difficult to get rid of a tea stain.'

'It is my fault. It was the surprise. I'm sorry.'

'Yes,' said Anthea. She repeated absently, 'Yes, it was, so it was.'

'I am so sorry.'

'Don't do that. Don't apologise! *She* was always apologising . . .'

'She? You mean Mrs. Haslett? Oh, I mustn't keep calling her that! Andrew says I must call her—but, no, I can't! I find it so difficult to call her Juliet.'

'Juliet . . .' Anthea's eyes filled with tears. 'I wonder if you know? I wonder if you are watching up there, what your feelings can be . . .'

'Oh, it is a surprise—a shock! I thought you knew. It should not have happened like this. And maybe it is that you don't approve? You are displeased?'

'I really don't know what to say! I am so astonished —I haven't quite taken it in . . . But it was wrong of him, very wrong not to have told me! After all, I had a right, he might at least have consulted me—it's so soon—he might have considered the effect this would have on his family, or his friends even, for that matter.'

'I don't know why he did not tell you. I do not understand.'

'Oh, I think I understand, I think I'm beginning to. I know him so much better than you do, my dear—for all that you may be his wife—I have known him so much longer, longer than anyone. Andrew is not all that you might . . . Oh, no, I mustn't say it, not when you are so newly married—oh, dear, I don't know when I'll get used to that one, I really can't think of him as having a wife other than Juliet!—but it would be uncharitable in me if at this stage, the tender beginnings, I tried to point out to you some of his weaknesses. I daresay you'll find them out for yourself soon enough.'

'It is not right that we should be talking about him like this. He would not like it if he knew I was discussing him with one of his sisters.'

'So that's how it is? He warned you? Oh, he's a sly one, very sly! And I know perfectly well why he sprang this surprise on me—though very awkward for you, my dear, I should have thought he would have had more consideration for *you*! But that's Andrew—oh, I know him backwards—going his own way, arranging things to his own satisfaction without giving a thought to other people! I know perfectly well that he did this to get his own back on me for having stayed so long in the house . . . Dear, dear, dear, what a bolt from the blue! I wonder how Frances will take it? And it's so near her time, too—only another month. It would be dreadful if the shock . . . You did know that she and Juliet were very friendly? Poor Juliet, hardly cold in the ground and, dying, too, in such sad circumstances!'

'Oh, I knew it would be like this!' Cara wrung her hands. 'I knew his family would not accept . . .'

'But, if you felt like that, why did you allow yourself to be ruled by him? A year at the very least— it would have been only decent—and even then it would have been rather soon, far too soon. And didn't it occur to you for the sake of your own reputation— did you ever stop to think how people might interpret it? After all, you had lived in the same house with them for a number of years . . .'

'Oh, that is not so! It is a wicked thing that you are saying! It is not true!'

'Well, I suppose I'll have to believe you, but I can't vouch for it that others will . . . Oh, it's all so complicated. And the children—such a disappointment. I had been so looking forward to . . .'

'But that is why we were married so soon. It was because of the children. We thought it would be best for them if it just happened quietly and naturally, with no awkward gap.'

'Those poor children . . .'

'But no! They are not poor children—they are quite contented. They are used to me, I've looked after them since they were babies. They have been my life ever since I was not a school-girl any more.'

'Yes, yes, my dear—don't excite yourself! I do understand. In fact I'm beginning to understand it all, it now seems so much less mysterious to me. It's obvious why Andrew married you—his children—it was the practical and convenient thing to do. It's not that he was looking for a substitute for Juliet . . . Yes, that makes it much more acceptable. And it must be easier for you, too, in that you won't need to feel that you are supplanting her or in any way offending against her memory.'

'You are telling me that he does not love me? Is it so?'

'Now, dear, that wasn't what I said—I never mentioned the word love. Nor will I. I wouldn't dream of intruding on,' she paused, 'on the intimate side of your relationship. So don't you go telling Andrew that

I've been filling your pretty head with nasty doubts. I won't have you believing me a monster! And now we'll change the subject, shall we? Your journey, was it pleasant—no hitches I trust, no little difficulties?'

'I . . . Excuse me—sometimes I have a difficulty with my English . . .'

'Oh, well, that won't do, will it, not now that you are married to an Englishman! Perhaps you had better go to language classes?'

'Oh, no, I have not made myself clear. It is not that I do not know how to make the words. It is something emotional, sometimes I . . .' She swallowed, then began afresh. 'I wish to thank you for all the pretty flowers. You have made the house so nice for us coming home. It will be sad for you, will it not, when you have to leave?'

'When I leave?'

'When you go to the country. Andrew told me you would be going to the country to that house whose name I can never pronounce.'

'That's the first I've heard of it! When does he expect this to happen?'

'Quite soon. He said he hoped already you would have been gone.'

'Really? You astonish me! What on earth does he expect of me? Does he think that after all these years I can suddenly pick myself up with a bundle and depart? My poor Andrew, if that's what he thinks he, too, will have a shock coming to him.'

'But he said you had re-furnished that house. He told me you had been living there all summer and you had said in your letters to him how it was delightful to be there.'

'Oh, that's a very different matter! As a summer place, a house for the holidays—we'll all go there during the school holidays.'

'No, no, he told me you are to live there and we are to live here.'

'But you won't want to live in this house! How cruel of Andrew! How can he expect you to live here after Juliet—the manner in which she died was so tragic . . . I mean, there was a doubt—I never believed that of course, not for one minute!—but it was said that it was not an accident. And it would be terrible for you to live here with such a shadow. Wouldn't you feel her memory reproaching you? Wouldn't you be afraid that Juliet might haunt the place?'

'Oh, no, Andrew says it is you who haunt this house!'

'Well!' Anthea gasped. When she had recovered her breath, she said: 'You seem such a quiet little person, but you're something of a dark horse, aren't you?' She got up and went over to the window. 'Oh, that lovely garden—how well I know it, every plant, every tree, they're companions of a life-time! He can't ask me to do it! He can't ask me to leave all this . . . Ah, Juliet, if only you were still with us! To think that it was only a year ago, almost to the day, when you came here—ah, how little did we know then—when you came to what was to be your last home on this earth . . . I can almost see you, walking there under the trees! Dearest Juliet, my poor, dear sister . . .' Her voice broke and she left the room sobbing piteously.

'What a happy sound!' Anthea entered the garden where Cara was playing with the children. 'How I love children's laughter—it does my heart good to hear them!'

'Good morning,' said Cara politely.

'And good morning to you, my dear! What a lovely morning it is—that gentle autumn sunlight! But still it is October . . . Now, I hope you won't think me interfering, but is it really warm enough for Lucy to be out without a coat?'

At a sign from Cara the little girl disappeared into the house and a moment later she was followed by her brothers.

'Are they frightened of me?' asked their aunt.

'They are a little shy of strangers.'

'Oh, dear—they'll have to get over that, won't they? Well, I must say you certainly have a way with them. I was watching you playing with them from my bedroom window.'

'Yes, they wanted to see the garden. I was showing them the fountain.'

'Ah, the fountain . . . And tell me, how do you like your garden?'

'My garden?'

'Yes, now it is your garden—all this is yours.'

'Oh, I do not know what to say. Yesterday you made me feel . . .' Cara paused, embarrassed. 'Did you sleep well last night?'

'No, I'm afraid not. I had a bad night, really when I come to think of it I hardly slept at all. But it doesn't seem to have affected me, in fact I can't remember when I've last felt so cheerful.'

'Oh? Then that is good . . .'

'But you don't look very well. You're far too pale! Are you sure that you had enough for breakfast?'

'I'm afraid I cannot eat your English breakfasts . . . But, no, it is not that that is making me feel . . .'

'What is it, dear? Is something the matter? Perhaps I can help—people always come to Anthea with their little worries.'

'Well . . . Since you ask me I must tell you that, yes, I am troubled—this situation, it is so perplexing. You see, I hadn't realised that Andrew had not told you about us. I hadn't known that you had planned to go on living here—oh, forgive me, I'm not saying this the right way, I don't mean to be offensive.'

'You want me to go?'

'No, no—you misunderstand! I have no wish for you to go. It is I who do not wish to stay. It is all so changed. I had thought this house so beautiful but now I do not like it at all that it should be mine. It is not because of *her*—she did not live here so long—it is because of you. He was right when he said that you—no, not haunted, but . . . How could I be happy here when I knew that you had been forced to leave because of me?'

'Now, now, dear, you're not to talk like that. What would Andrew say? He's not going to change his plans, not at this stage—he's so determined. And why shouldn't he be? It is his house and it's only right that he should . . . And it will be so nice for the children, it's a family house, and they will make it come to life again. You'll get used to it after you've been settled in for a while.'

'But you? You will not want to leave? Those things you said, you were so upset . . .'

'Ah, yes, but I was suffering from—if you'll forgive me, dear—from shock. I was so taken aback. I really couldn't collect my thoughts together at all. You see, I had been waiting to discuss it all, our domestic arrangements, with Andrew when he arrived. I had imagined—I had hoped—that he would want me to look after his children for him, I'm very fond of children, you know, very much a creature of hearth and home, and I felt so sorry for the poor little things having lost their mother while they were still so young . . . So you can understand my confusion when you told me that you and he were married. It was so totally unexpected!'

'Oh, yes, I can quite . . .'

'Now, dear, don't look so distressed—you're not to worry yourself on my account. You see, I've had a whole night to think it over, to get used to the idea, and I'll tell you what's going to happen. You're going to live here with Andrew and you're going to enjoy it and you're not to give a second thought to me. I shall go to Cheyncotes as he planned. Really, what an idiot he is—if he'd only told me he was bringing home a new wife to this house, why, I'd have left at once! Still as it is things haven't turned out too badly. I've kept the place warm for you and my own move shouldn't present too many difficulties as the other house is all ready for us. I'll just stay a few days longer to collect my things together and perhaps in the meantime I can help you find your way around, show you where things are in the house, how we manage the laundry and so on, where to shop locally.'

'But you confuse me! You are too good, too generous!'

'Not at all, my dear! Oh, I won't say it was easy to adjust myself, but when it was done it was done, and, as you'll no doubt discover, once I've made up my mind about something there's little in heaven and earth that can make me change it.'

'But this has happened—you have changed so suddenly, I find it hard to understand . . .'

'Oh, you will understand when you know me, when you know us better—we Hasletts are pretty resilient!' Anthea smiled at her: 'Cara—that means dear one, doesn't it? How well the name suits you, you are such a good, kind girl . . . You know, when I was thinking about you last night I came to the conclusion that there is really no one in the world who could be a more fitting replacement for poor Juliet, and I'm sure she would agree with me herself, she was so very fond of you. And it will be fun for the children to have someone young . . . I hope you won't mind it, dear, if I think of you more as a daughter than as a sister? You really belong to a different generation . . . Ah, Cara, how happy I am that you should become one of my dear ones!' She kissed her and the girl, taken by surprise, trembled. 'How white you've gone! Are you afraid of me? You mustn't be frightened of me—not silly old Anthea, no one could possibly be frightened of her!'

'Oh, you must excuse me! I am not quite myself. You see, I had thought you didn't want me here and now you are being so good to me that I am quite overwhelmed . . . But if you do go, surely it will be a sad thing for you?'

'Well, life is very strange . . . You know, I had thought I would never be able to leave this house,

I just couldn't contemplate it, thought it would break my heart—and yet now that it's actually come to the point I'm rather excited by the idea of a change. How right Andrew is! He always used to say that change was beneficial for its own sake . . . I suppose,' she glanced slyly at the new wife, 'he must still believe in change?'

'Oh,' Cara blushed, 'yes, I have heard him say he thought it was a good thing.'

'It certainly is as far as I'm concerned. I've made myself so comfortable here that I'd really become a terrible old stick in the mud, never going anywhere or doing anything interesting. But now life opens up all sorts of possibilities. Why, I was thinking I might even travel—it's such years since I went abroad. I shall certainly come with you when you next visit the Italian lakes, you'll be going quite soon, won't you?'

'Oh, I don't know that that was what Andrew . . .'

'Perhaps you'll wait till the spring when the weather's better? Never mind, it's not as if I was unable to occupy myself in the meantime. I shall find plenty to do at Cheyncotes—I've got all sorts of plans about that! Now I'll tell you what I've been thinking. I've always been the home-maker in this family, it's second nature to me and I don't see any reason why that should change. I know this is a lovely house and in London it's so nice to have a garden, but there will be times when you will want to get away from it, from the city—if only for the sake of the children as the country will be so much healthier for them. So I've decided that Cheyncotes will be the house where you'll spend the school holidays. I've got it all worked out, where you're going to sleep and the children can all use the same play-room . . . And there's no reason why you shouldn't come during term-time. Now that you're living in London you'll find that all Londoners like to get away for the odd weekend. So what do you say to that? Or perhaps I should ask you what will Andrew say?'

'I'm not sure . . . No, I must be honest with you—that was not what he had planned. I am sorry but I do not think he will want to go to the country.'

'But you'll persuade him,' Anthea pressed the hand of her new sister-in-law, 'I can count on that, can't I? Now I'll tell you what we'll do, we'll start this Christmas—Christmas is such fun when there's a large family. As soon as I go down there I'm going to get it all arranged, I shall order the Christmas tree and the decorations—and just think of it, the five little cousins opening their presents together on Christmas morning! Isn't that a jolly idea?'

'Oh, yes, it is! But . . .'

'There! I knew it would appeal to you. And as for the "buts" . . . Well, poor Andrew, I suppose he'll feel he'll never get away from that wretched bossy sister of his? But then neither he will! Besides,' she smiled serenely, 'he can't have things all his own way. That wouldn't be quite fair, would it, dear?'